"I Don't Want To Hurt You."

He paused. "And I don't want you falling in love with me and then one day waking up and realizing I'm not the man you wanted me to be."

"So where does that leave us?" she asked, her tone tinged with defiance.

He shrugged. "We'll still work together."

"I meant where does this leave us personally? You're convinced I'm some delicate flower who can't handle being involved with you. But you're wrong. I can handle anything."

He smiled at her bravado. And her choice of words. He should probably just calmly walk away from that innuendo, but, damn it, he couldn't. "Am I to assume you want to handle me?"

Dear Reader,

It's always a thrill to work on a continuity. For starters, it's a huge honor to work with so many of the authors whose work I admire. Working on a continuity also helps me stretch and grow as a writer. For example, the hero of this story, Ward Miller, is a musician. Rock star is not a profession I would have picked for a hero all on my own, yet I ended up having a blast writing about Ward.

I live near Austin, Texas, which is known as the Live Music Capital of the World. One of my favorite local muscians is a guitarist and singer named Monte Montgomery. When I gave a voice to Ward, it was Monte's music that I heard in my mind. If you want to hear Ward…um, I mean Monte, check out "Love Come Knockin'" or "When Will I." They're all available on iTunes.

I hope you enjoy this book and the whole continuity. As for me, I can't wait to read all the books in the series!

Emily McKay

EMILY McKAY

SEDUCED: THE UNEXPECTED VIRGIN

Published by Silhouette Books
America's Publisher of Contemporary Romance

Special thanks and acknowledgment to Emily McKay for her contribution to The Takeover miniseries.

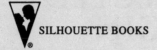 SILHOUETTE BOOKS

ISBN-13: 978-0-373-73079-7

Recycling programs for this product may not exist in your area.

SEDUCED: THE UNEXPECTED VIRGIN

Books by Emily McKay

EMILY McKAY

has been reading romance novels since she was eleven years old. Her first Harlequin Romance came free in a box of Hefty garbage bags. She has been reading and loving romance novels ever since. She lives in Texas with her geeky husband, her two kids and too many pets. Her debut novel, *Baby, Be Mine,* was a RITA® Award finalist for Best First Book and Best Short Contemporary. She was a 2009 *RT Book Reviews* Career Achievement nominee for Series Romance. You can hang out with her online at the eHarlequin site, JauntyQuills.com or her website, www.EmilyMcKay.com.

This book is—quite naturally—for all the musicians whose music I love and listen to obsessively in the final stages of writing my books. In particular, Nancy Giffith, for her poignant lyrics and her ability to tell a story with more emotional resonance in three minutes than I can tell in 240 pages. And Monte Montgomery, for giving a sound and voice to Ward.

* * *

Don't miss a single book in this series!

The Takeover
For better, for worse. For business, for pleasure.
These tycoons have vowed to have it all!

Claimed: The Pregnant Heiress by Day Leclaire
Seduced: The Unexpected Virgin by Emily McKay
Revealed: His Secret Child by Sandra Hyatt
Bought: His Temporary Fiancée by Yvonne Lindsay
Exposed: Her Undercover Millionaire by Michelle Celmer
Acquired: The CEO's Small-Town Bride by Catherine Mann

One

The last thing Ana Rodriguez needed in her life was another preening, self-indulgent star. Mere weeks ago, she'd walked away from her successful career as a costume designer in Hollywood for precisely that reason. So when her best friend, Emma Worth, had suggested she apply for the job as the director for a charity starting up in her hometown of Vista del Mar, Ana had jumped at the chance.

A fresh start was just what she needed. Away from the drama of Hollywood. Away from stars who would make her life miserable just because she didn't put out.

Since then, she'd found out she'd be working with Ward Miller, a musical superstar who glowed brighter than anyone she'd known in Hollywood. In her experience, the bigger the name, the bigger the ego. Only now, instead of merely dressing the megalomaniac, she had to pander to his every need, listen to his opinions, take his advice and generally make sure he was thrilled to be the celebrity face of the charity, Hannah's Hope.

With a critical eye, she scanned the charity's humble front office. As their mission statement said, they provided "mentoring and resources for disadvantaged individuals." Which was a fancy way of saying "We help poor people." In general, Ana wasn't fond of fancy ways of saying things.

"You're stewing," a friendly voice chided.

Ana looked over her shoulder to Christi Cox, her assistant director. "I'm not stewing. I'm mulling."

Which was just a fancy way of saying "stewing." Ana uncrossed her arms to toy with the delicate trio of golden loops that comprised her earrings.

The furnishings of the front room were clean, but strictly utilitarian. Functional worktables supplemented with used chairs and bookshelves she'd picked up on Craigslist. The conference room, offices and kitchen in back were even less chic. She'd sent Omar, Hannah's Hope's third employee, out to the grocery store to buy coffee. But she doubted even the most gourmet of brews would impress Miller.

She'd dressed up the front room as best she could, with some throw pillows, a floor lamp—to soften the glare of overhead fluorescents—and a bright throw rug, all items she'd had at home. They reflected her eclectic style and added a touch of comfort to the room, but no elegance.

In short, the facilities for Hannah's Hope looked exactly like what they were: fifty percent meeting space, fifty percent classroom, one hundred percent last, best hope for its clientele. Zero percent schmooze room for spoiled celebrities.

She couldn't shake the fear that Miller would walk in here and turn his nose up at all they'd done. But underneath that was a deeper fear. That he'd walk in here, have one conversation with her and realize she was a fraud who lacked the skills to make Hannah's Hope really soar.

If anyone could see through her, it was Miller. He wasn't just a musical god, he was also legendary for his charitable work on behalf of the Cara Miller Foundation, an organization he'd started after the death of his wife. He'd donated and raised countless millions. He sat on the board of more charities than she could count, including the newly formed board of Hannah's Hope.

And the truth was, she'd gotten this job only because Emma also sat on the board. Growing up with Emma was practically her sole qualification for being the director of Hannah's Hope.

The hopes and dreams of the entire town rested on her shoulders. She didn't dare let them down. Not when they needed her so desperately.

Besides, she needed this job. Not just because she'd quit her other one. Not because she'd invested all her savings in a tiny bungalow in one of Vista del Mar's middle-class neighborhoods. But because after four years of draping fabric and making beautiful people look good, she needed to do something important. She needed to make a difference.

If only she had more time to get her feet under her before Miller showed up. It was bad enough that she felt so horribly unprepared for this job, why did she have to deal with him so early in her stint as director? Rafe Cameron, the charity's founder, was an inattentive board member at best. Rafe—hometown bad boy turned corporate raider—was focused on taking over Worth Industries, the company that fueled the local economy. Rafe had started Hannah's Hope to create goodwill within the community, but Ana suspected he was motivated more by public relations spin than true benevolence. Emma supported her one hundred percent. But Ward was the wild card. Would he swoop in and perform the kind of miracle he had for the Cara Miller Foundation? Or was he merely Rafe's watchdog, sent here to judge her every misstep?

Besides, he was Ward freakin' Miller. Musical superstar and the most recognizable do-gooder in the country. Oh, yeah. And he was hot.

Any one of those elements would be enough to intimidate a woman of her meager accomplishments. The triple whammy just might induce cardiac arrest.

Maybe she was even hoping he'd turn out to be a jerk. She'd been a fan of his since she hit puberty. Professional distance would be easier to fake if he ended up being just as obnoxious as…oh, say, Ridley Sinclair, the supposedly happily married movie star who'd relentlessly hit on her. Okay, so Ward didn't have to be *that* bad. All she asked for was just a smidge of artistic temperament to help her establish some boundaries between her fantasies of Ward and the real-life man she was about to face.

Christi came to stand beside Ana. They stood shoulder to shoulder by their office door, trying to imagine the first impression the room would give.

Ana clucked. "It's not fancy enough. It's not elegant enough. We should have met at the Vista Del Mar Beach and Tennis Club like I wanted to."

"His personal assistant said he didn't expect any special treatment," Christi reminded her.

Ana gave a guffaw of disbelief. "I've worked with a lot of famous people. They all expect special treatment."

And she was *so* not good at pandering to celebrities. Inevitably, she tired of their nonsense and her temper got the better of her. *Oh, it's that fiery Latin temper,* her friends would tease. Which only made it worse. She hated living down to that stereotype.

"Either they demand a particular kind of water, chilled to a precise temperature," she continued. "Or they want a collection of seventeen different snacks that are all a shade of blue. Or they're on some cleansing diet that requires them to snort free-range kelp up their nose five times a day."

"I think," Christi quipped, "I would have remembered it if his assistant had mentioned free-range kelp snorting."

"What *did* the assistant mention?" Ana asked, unable to swallow her curiosity any longer. "Never mind. I don't want to know."

She wasn't a groupie scanning the pages of *Tiger Beat* for the Jonas Brothers' favorite color of M&M. This was professional interest only.

But it irritated her that she asked, because of course she *was* curious. What hot-blooded American woman between the ages of twenty and eighty-nine wouldn't be? What woman her age hadn't slow danced in some smoky bar to the sonorous rhythm of "Falling Hard"? Or sat in traffic singing along with "Caught You"?

He was her generation's…well, Bono, Paul McCartney and

Johnny Cash all rolled into one. A sexy bad boy with a heart of pure platinum and talent for writing songs so good they made your soul ache. He hadn't performed or put out any new albums since his wife, Cara, had died of cancer three years ago. His absence from the public eye only added to his mystique. Die-hard fans still clamored for new songs. She certainly had her share of giddy excitement about meeting him. Maybe more than her share. But she'd worked really hard to bury it under a layer of professionalism. She just hoped she succeeded.

She glanced at her watch again. "And, he's officially late. Very late."

Then a voice came from behind her. "Not too late, I hope."

It was the gravelly voice of a rock star, a voice she'd know anywhere. Hearing it made her stomach drop straight down to her toes.

She turned slowly toward the voice. And there he was. Ward Miller.

He stood just inside the hallway that led to the service entrance. He was taller than she expected, maybe just shy of six feet. He dressed in the ubercasual style of celebrities, with green cargo pants and a simple V-neck white T-shirt that emphasized the breadth of his shoulders. He held mirrored aviator glasses in one hand and had on a Stingrays ball cap. Why did stars always think a simple hat would be enough to fool people? His dark, wavy hair was shorter than when he'd toured regularly, but still long enough to make him look scruffy and a little disreputable. His face was narrow, his lips thin, but neither feature made him look parsimonious, as they might have on another man. Instead, he looked soulful and sensitive. Though not entirely tamed. That edge of wildness surprised her. Magazine photos hadn't captured that.

Perhaps most important, he didn't look offended. Good thing, too. Hardworking do-gooders with liberal arts degrees were a dime a dozen, but mega rock stars willing to lend their name to a charity were *so* much harder to come by.

Face-to-face with all his star power, she suddenly felt a little light-headed. "Mr. Miller, you've surprised us by sneaking in the service entrance." She hadn't intended to let the note of censure creep into her voice. But maybe that was better than the alternative. She could all too easily imagine herself giggling like a schoolgirl.

"I hope you don't mind. The paparazzi followed us from the airport. I'm sorry I'm late." And then, he winked at her. "I didn't even have time to pick up any free-range kelp."

Ward waited for the enticing brunette to laugh at his teasing—after all, her quip about snorting kelp had nearly had him guffawing. He didn't meet many people willing to laugh at his fame. It was refreshing.

Instead, her posture stiffened making her appear slightly taller than he'd first thought, though she still couldn't have been more than five-six. She blushed, which made her skin glow a gorgeous peach. With her luxurious tumble of dark hair, her wide smile and her high cheekbones, she looked lushly exotic.

However, she was also simmering with anger.

"Sorry I had to sneak in the back," he said, trying again to massage her into a more amiable frame of mind. "We made it all the way to the San Diego airport unnoticed. But Drew Barrymore and that guy from the Apple ads were there, flying off on some vacation. Unfortunately, they made it through security just as we were coming out, so there was already a swarm of photographers there."

He made light of it, but SUVs of camera-toting leeches had followed for nearly thirty miles. His driver had almost lost them in the maze of streets in the business district of Vista del Mar. In fact, his assistant and publicist had stayed in the car when he hopped out, both to speed things up and in hopes that the paparazzi would see the figures still in the back of the car and keep following it.

Since Ana didn't seem amused by his joke, he flashed a smile at her companion. The woman returned his smile faintly. She had that fluttery look fans sometimes got.

He extended his hand. "Hi, I'm Ward Miller."

"Hi," the older blonde woman said in a breathy voice, before clearing her throat. "I'm Christi Cox. I'm the assistant director here at Hannah's Hope." As she slipped her hand in his, she gave a giggly squeak and elbowed Ana in the side. "See, he's not pretentious or preening."

Christi returned his wink with an exaggerated one of her own. Instantly, he liked her. He wasn't going to have any trouble getting along with her. The jury was still out on the prickly other woman.

She stepped forward and extended her own hand along with a tight smile. "I'm Ana Rodriguez. The director of Hannah's Hope."

She shook his hand for only an instant before she pulled it back and tucked it close to her side. Good thing he hadn't been expecting any more warmth in the greeting.

With a frown, she nodded toward the window. "It looks like you didn't do such a good job shaking them after all."

He looked out the front window at the street beyond. A white SUV sat in front of the building, parked at a haphazard angle. A second later, another SUV squealed to a halt beside the first. And then a third.

His cell phone vibrated and then hummed the seven-note bridge in the "Falling Hard" ringtone his aunt bought him for his birthday last year as a joke.

Ana's brows snapped together in a frown at the sound of his phone ringing. Automatically, he glanced down at the caller ID. It was Jess, his assistant. "I better take this. He won't be long."

"Sorry, man," Jess launched into speech without preamble or introduction. "We lost them at the hotel. I told Ryan we should keep driving, but he was eager to check in."

"No worries," Ward said into the phone, keeping his tone casual. Ryan, Ward's publicist, could steamroll the pope. And since he was a believer in the old as-long-as-they-spell-your-name-right axiom, Ryan had probably demanded he and Jess check into the hotel precisely to engineer the press finding Ward. "You guys get settled in there. I'll text you when I want you to send the car back."

He ended the call and slid the phone back in his pocket with a pained smile. "Well, looks like they're here to stay. Shall we go out and answer some questions?" He gave her shoulder a friendly clap. She looked at him with such surprise, he found himself leaving his hand there. "If we throw them a bone, maybe they'll leave us alone."

For a moment, he had the urge to slide his hand to the nape of her neck. Before he could stop himself, he did. With a gentle touch, he steered her toward the door. "Come on, let's get out there."

She skittered away from his touch. "Why should *I* go?"

"Free press is good press. Might as well make this work for Hannah's Hope."

"I—" Then she broke off, seeming to consider his words. "I guess you're right." With a shrug, she approached the door, carefully slanting her shoulders so she slipped through the door.

However, her thick, long hair nearly brushed his chest as she passed. Her hair smelled warm and fragrant. Like cinnamon left in the sun. A breeze drifted in through the open door, mixing her scent with the briny tang of the ocean. It was like eating snickerdoodles at the beach.

Longing stabbed at him, so sharp it nearly sucked the air out of the room. The combination was both homey and exotic. Welcoming and erotic.

It was a damn inconvenient time for his body to respond so strongly to a woman.

At least he didn't have to worry about getting his heart involved, as well. As he'd sat at Cara's deathbed, he'd made a promise to himself. He'd never love again.

Cameras snapped the instant Ward stepped outside. As a recent denizen of Hollywood, Ana was no stranger to the buzz of gossipmongers. If there was one thing her four years in the movie biz had taught her, it was that celebrities came alive in front of the camera and lived for the attention of the press.

Ward's attitude only reaffirmed that impression. She barely had a chance to acclimate to the horde of reporters stewing on the street. And, good Lord, where had they all come from? She would have sworn they arrived in clown cars, rather than SUVs.

However, Ward was already smiling with practiced ease and answering questions with a rakish smile.

"No, today is just a business meeting," he was saying. He started to gesture toward Ana.

She had an instant of hoping he'd steer the questions toward Hannah's Hope. Readying herself to step forward and talk, she gave her slim skirt a tug, secretly longing for the familiarity of the more flamboyant clothes she wore when she wasn't trying to look so professional. But then a brunette from the back of the crowd edged her way forward. Ana recognized Gillian Mitchell, a reporter from the local paper, the *Seaside Gazette*. She called out a question. "I heard you'd booked time at a recording studio up in L.A. Are you working on a new album?"

"Of course, there's always a possibility I'll return to my recording career." He rolled up onto the balls of his feet.

With his hands tucked into his pants pockets, he exuded a sort of good ol' boy, aw-shucks enthusiasm that implied that *possibility* was more of a reality. "But for now I'm just producing an album with a local musician, Dave Summers, who just signed with my label. It's important for me to let other young musicians have the same opportunities that I had." Then he leaned a little closer and winked at the reporter. "But a songwriter is always a songwriter. I still have stories to tell."

Ana tried to resist rolling her eyes. Her lips felt stiff from the forced smile, her teeth brittle from biting back her sarcasm. Sneaked in the back, indeed. He'd probably engineered this whole thing. What a jerk.

Finally, just as some of the reporters were starting to drift off, he said, "But it's my work for charity that brings me here today. Let me tell you about Hannah's Hope…."

Ana tried to smile with more enthusiasm now. The charity he'd started in honor of his wife, the Cara Miller Foundation, was world-renowned for its work with underprivileged children. Though CMF had no formal relationship with Hannah's Hope,

Ward was a board member for both organizations. He was known for his philanthropic works, and was reclusive enough that any appearances piqued the public's interest. At the appropriate moment, she said a sentence or two about the services Hannah's Hope provided and their mission statement. She'd barely had a chance to rattle off the web address when the first of the cars loaded up and pulled out.

As the last of the reporters wandered off, she turned to look at Ward. His expression was tight, his lips pressed into a thin line of strain. For a second, she wondered whether this had been harder on him than he'd let on. But then he caught her looking at him and he smiled.

That smile, so up close and personal, seemed to suck the air right out of her lungs. She felt that same heady breathlessness she had when he'd introduced himself earlier. Like her blood had suddenly warmed by a few degrees.

"That went well," he said, flashing those white teeth at her like the barely tamed big bad wolf his press kit made him out to be.

She caught herself wanting to simper in response. Self-consciously, she ran a hand over her hair. She dropped her hand to her side as soon as she realized what she was doing. She would not be distracted by him. No matter how charming he was.

"Just great," she said with forced cheer.

He raised his eyebrows, his steady gaze unnerving her. "Is it all celebrities you don't like or is it just me? Because if you have a problem with me, I'd rather know it now." After a moment, he cocked his head toward her just slightly, lending a sense of intimacy to the hushed conversation. There had been a subtle sexual undercurrent to all his words. The gentle teasing, the low voice, the heat of his hand on her neck.

She'd seen stars do this before. Manipulate and coax people into doing exactly what they wanted. With female stars, it came across as a sort of chummy friendliness. A subtle "Let's be best buds!" vibe. With men, there was always a sensual promise to the overtures. An "I'll take you to bed and pleasure you beyond your wildest imaginings" implication.

She'd spent too long in Hollywood to be fooled by such tactics. Despite that, she felt a stirring of heat deep in her belly. Her body responding to the promise her mind knew was just a ruse.

And maybe that irritated her most of all. She knew better, yet despite all her big talk, she was still vulnerable. She still felt the powerful pull of attraction to him. The part of her that had grown up as a Ward Miller fan desperately wanted him to like her. Moreover, that part of her desperately wanted him to be likable. Despite the fact that she knew how unlikely that was.

She had to muster her indignation.

"You're right. I don't like celebrities. And what happened out there is a perfect example why. If you're going to talk about Hannah's Hope, then talk about the program." She stepped forward, closing the distance between them and then immediately wishing she hadn't. Dang, but he smelled good. "Don't use us as a platform for launching your comeback. The work we do is too important. There are people who really need our services and if you climb over them to get into the limelight, then you're—" She stumbled then over her words, her tirade foiled by her own expectations. Swallowing past the last remnants of her fantasies, she forced out her words. "Then you're not the man I thought you were."

Two

At the height of his career, when he'd traveled more than two hundred days a year, Ward had been able to float between time zones with only an extra shot of caffeine to get him going. Either he was getting older or his time out of the circuit had changed him. He'd flown into San Diego from visiting a charity in Texas that CMF was involved with. However, despite the fact that he was only two time zones away, he woke up at four local time and couldn't go back to sleep.

So he'd rolled out of bed, dressed for a jog on the beach, and had headed out in the early-morning gloom before getting so much as a whiff of coffee. He knew he'd feel the effects of getting less than six hours sleep later in the day, but he figured getting up was better than lying there tormenting himself.

He dressed quickly in sweatpants, a T-shirt and his jogging shoes.

His condo in Vista del Mar sat on a deserted stretch of beach. His assistant, Jess, had come out for a couple of days the previous week to rent the modest one bedroom condo. Though many larger rentals had been available, Ward had opted for compact and close to the water, glad to have the excuse to put Jess and Ryan up at the hotel rather than having them stay with him. He valued his privacy too much to want them underfoot. This time of morning, only the most stalwart of beachgoers would be out. By the time he was jogging along the beach, the faintest hint of light was creeping over the horizon chasing away the night. It would be another hour before the sun rose. For now, he was alone with the sand under his pounding feet, the surf roaring in his ears, and the breeze biting his cheeks. Still, it wasn't quite enough to block out the memory of her words.

Not the man I thought you were.

There was enough punch in that one sentence to cripple a man.

He'd disappointed a lot of people in his life. People who'd relied on him. People he'd loved. Was it really too much to ask of himself that he not disappoint this one, fiery-tempered do-gooder?

Hell, maybe it wouldn't have been so bad if it was merely his inconvenient and unexpected attraction to Ana Rodriguez that kept him awake. Sexual attraction came and went. It was a simple truth in his life that women were—and always had been—plentiful. There'd even been times, before Cara, that he'd indulged in the cornucopia of femininity that his career presented him with. He'd learned enough restraint since then that merely being attracted to Ana didn't bother him.

The real problem was, some tiny part of him feared that Ana looked right through him to his very soul and saw the truth. That he really wouldn't live up to her expectations. He never did.

He could shove aside everything else. He was good at burying his emotions these days. But he couldn't make himself forget that.

When Cara died, he'd lost himself briefly in his grief. He'd managed to fight, tooth and nail, to get back to himself. To climb out of his despair and rebuild his life without her. But the truth was, he'd done it by following one simple principle. Keep moving.

It was like jogging. You just put one foot ahead of the other.

You never give yourself permission to think. You just move.
You forget the pain streaming through your muscles. Forget the
blisters forming on your heels. Forget the anguish of watching
a loved one being eaten alive by cancer and not being able to do
a damn thing to stop it. You just move.

And if you're fast enough and you don't ever stop, you somehow manage to stay in front of it.

For the past three years, he'd worked eighteen-hour days
getting the Cara Miller Foundation started and running smoothly.
He'd contacted every wealthy or influential person he'd ever met
and hit them up for support or donations. He'd found work that
he was passionate about and he'd devoted himself to doing it.

He'd visited other charities. He'd studied the way they were
run. He'd learned from them, revamped their models. And started
over again. Never staying in any one place long enough to catch
his breath. He'd worked tirelessly. He'd done it in honor of his
wife's memory. But he'd also done it because it helped him forget
her.

It was a dichotomy he wasn't sure he was ready to contemplate
during a morning run on the beach. His muscles burned and
his joints ached as his feet ate up mile after mile. But he still
kept on jogging, slowly acknowledging that Ana was certainly
right about one thing. Hannah's Hope needed him, but it needed
him for more than a quick stop off on the way to some other
destination. If he was going to help Hannah's Hope, it needed
to be more than drive-by charity work.

Jogging was the one thing that cleared his head. The one
thing that blocked out all the nonsense. Music had been that way
for him once. Back before Cara got sick. But cancer had taken
not only his wife but every musical urge he had. There'd been a
time when he couldn't go a day without playing the guitar. When
songs had teased at the edges of his mind no matter what he was
doing. All that was gone. Now all he had was jogging. But you
couldn't run forever. Sooner or later, you had to stop, catch your
breath and turn around to go home.

So Ward slowed his steps. He stopped for a moment, braced
his palms on his knees and bent over to suck in deep lungfuls of

salty air. Then he turned around and started for the condo. But he didn't run there. He walked the rest of the way. By the time the condo was in sight, the sun was peeking over the rooftops across the street from the beach. He was just in time for the sunrise.

Ana arrived at Hannah's Hope late the following day after a very discouraging meeting at the bank. Sure, they had plenty of money—for now—but more paperwork was the last thing she needed right now. Especially since the paperwork required involved signatures from board members. While Rafe was always willing to sign papers, it sometimes took days for him to get around to it. Since she needed the papers by morning, someone from Hannah's Hope would have to drive over to Worth Industries and wait around for Rafe to actually get a pen in his hand during a free moment. And just now that felt like time she didn't have to spare.

As she let herself in the back door of Hannah's Hope, juggling her briefcase and purse, she called out, "I'm not really here. I'm just dropping off my laptop on my way over to…"

She let her voice trail off as she glanced around the back room and realized no one was there to hear her explanation. Where was everyone?

Usually by this late in the morning, both Christi and Omar were there. She stuck her head through the doorway of the office they shared, but found it empty. She set down her laptop on her desk chair and followed the sound of voices to the conference room.

She took in the scene before her in one rapid sweep. Christi and Omar were seated on the near side of the conference table. Emma Worth sat up at the head of the table, her own laptop open in front of her. One arm was still encased in a purple cast from a recent car accident, so she was typing one-handed. A bowl of fresh fruit sat in the center of the table, as well as a tray of pastries and muffins wrapped in the Bistro by the Sea's signature bright blue papers. A box of their coffee sat on the bookshelf with a stack of paper cups. The divinely pungent scent of coffee filled the air, with the subtle undernotes of blueberry muffins.

Obviously, someone had decided to have breakfast catered in. And she suspected that same person was currently standing at the front of the room writing on the whiteboard.

Ward was dressed in jeans and a plaid flannel shirt. His back was to her as he wrote, but she could tell by the way the fabric draped that it was unbuttoned. Probably to hang open over some muscle-sculpting T-shirt that would drive her to distraction. His wavy hair curled over the back of his collar, making her fingers itch to run through those curls.

She hissed out a breath through her clenched teeth. Prying her jaw open, she asked, "What exactly is going on here?"

Three heads swiveled in her direction. Christi and Omar smiled broadly. Emma's gaze darted away nervously like she knew Ana wouldn't approve.

Ward's hand stilled midword. Then slowly he turned to face her. His smile was slow, lazy and just a bit smug.

And damn it, yep, there was the maroon, chest-hugging shirt. Just what she expected. It took a hell of a man to make mere denim, cotton and flannel look elegant, but somehow Ward pulled it off. Batman in a tux didn't look this good.

"Good," he said. "You're just in time. We're brainstorming."

"Where'd the food come from?"

"That little restaurant downtown. What's it called?"

"The Bistro," Emma said sheepishly.

"Yes." He nodded. "Bistro by the Sea. Great little place. I brought the food in."

"And the whiteboards?" she asked pointedly. Whiteboards had been on their want-to-buy-soon-but-not-yet-in-our-budget list.

His smile broadened. "Guilty as charged."

There were two of them. They hadn't yet been installed, but rested against four of the chairs that had been dragged in from the other room. At the top of one were the words *What we need*. On the other, the words *How to get it*. Funny, she didn't see catered meals under either column.

"Wasn't it nice of Ward to bring us muffins?" Emma asked, her tone overly bright.

"So generous, I hardly know what to say," she muttered drily.

The skin around his eyes crinkled with barely suppressed humor, as if he read the subtle sarcasm she'd tried to keep from her voice. "You're welcome." He gestured toward the bounty on the table—more than any five people could eat in one morning. "Why don't you pour yourself a cup of coffee and join us. We're just getting started."

"I can't." She held up the portfolio of documents. "I'll be spending most of the day in Rafe's office, so he can sign these papers by tomorrow. Actually, I need signatures from you two, as well." She slid the folder toward Emma. "If you could sign it before I leave, that would be perfect."

"I'm meeting Rafe for dinner tonight," Ward said easily as he crossed to stand directly across from her on the other side of the table. "I'll take the papers and have him sign them."

Ana snatched up the portfolio before Ward could take it. "That's not necessary."

Still, he reached for it and grabbed the corner. "It's not a big deal."

Both of their arms stretched out across the table, each holding an edge of the folder. Suddenly, they were no longer debating which of them would ask Rafe to sign the papers. They were fighting over control of Hannah's Hope. Letting him take the papers would be admitting she couldn't do her job. Yet, fighting over it made her seem like a controlling bitch.

She was painfully aware of the others' gazes bouncing back and forth between them. Aware of Ward's easy, confident smile. And of the tight strain of hers. She'd already lost the battle.

"Great," she said, pushing the folder toward him. "Just make sure I have it first thing in the morning."

Ward set the portfolio down on the table and once again gestured to the empty chair at the table. "Take a seat. I'm eager to hear your thoughts."

As she lowered herself to the chair, she noticed a crisp blank writing tablet sitting in front of her, a new pen propped on top. A glance around the table showed her that everyone had pads. Christi and Omar had already started taking notes.

As the group tossed out more ideas, she carefully drew a line down the center of the top page and copied Ward's two headings What We Need and How to Get It.

So, what did she need?

More training.

More time to figure out how to do her job.

Less time with the sexy, but meddling rock star.

How to get it?

Under that column, she had nothing but question marks.

A few hours later—after Ward had taken them all to lunch at the Vista del Mar Beach and Tennis Club—Ana was finally able to retreat into her office to sulk. She maintained no illusions. Sulking was precisely what she was doing. During lunch, Emma had been in her element. Ana had eaten at the club often enough that she was no longer intimidated by the elegant atmosphere and sophisticated food. However, Christi and Omar were duly impressed. She tried to tell herself that enjoying their food was not a sign of betrayal. Her overly sensitive emotions didn't listen.

So by the time Emma knocked on the door and stuck her head into Ana's office, Ana was feeling surly and disgruntled.

Immediately reading Ana's mood, Emma asked, "Aren't you pleased with all we accomplished today? It feels like things are really starting to take off."

Ana shrugged noncommittally as she crossed her arms over her chest. And then quickly dropped them to her side. This was one of the disadvantages of working with someone who knew you so well.

Ana's parents had worked for the Worths for years. She'd spent her teenage years living in the apartment over their garage. Though Ana's family was hired help, Emma's kindness and generosity meant they hadn't been treated that way. Ana and Emma were practically sisters.

She tried not to be annoyed by Emma's cheerful demeanor. Within the past month, Emma had fallen in love with Chase Larson, Rafe's stepbrother. It certainly wasn't Emma's fault that she was practically glowing with the combination of love-infused happiness and pregnancy hormones. Of course she was happy for her friend. And yet, Ana couldn't help but feel Emma's new status as pregnant and soon-to-be-married only highlighted Ana's own perpetual and permanent state as a singleton.

But none of that had any relevance to Hannah's Hope.

Ana tapped her fingers on her desk. "It feels like a lot of big dreams that we aren't going to be able to do anything about."

Emma frowned at the unexpected censure. "Me, I'm thrilled." She took a sip from the bottle of water that she seemed to carry with her constantly now that she was pregnant. "I think we came up with a lot of great ideas. What about the street fair? Surely you love that idea."

Christi had thrown out the idea halfway through the brainstorming. Instead of hosting an open house next week on a weekday evening, they would host a street fair in downtown Vista del Mar at the end of the month. They could generate far more publicity as well as draw in plenty of passersby. Everyone else had loved the idea.

"It's not that it's a bad idea. But we still have so much real work to do to get Hannah's Hope off the ground. I'm still working with our accountant to file our 501(c)(3) application. I don't want us to get distracted planning something fun when there's serious work that needs to get done."

"This isn't a distraction." Emma's tone showed her excitement. "Now that we're up and running, how many people really know about us? We need to reach out to the community and let people see everything we have to offer, both to clients and to volunteers. This is the perfect way to do that."

"I'm not saying a street fair won't be fun, I'm just not sure it's the best use of our resources."

"That's the beauty of getting local businesses to donate goods and services. And if Ward really can get some up-and-coming local act to perform, we'll be golden."

Omar was the one who had brought up the possibility of Ward performing. Ward had smoothly dodged the question by offering up the services of the musician whose albums he was producing.

"Yeah, great." Here she was trying to play the taskmaster and get everyone to complete paperwork and Ward swept in with his fun ideas and yummy muffins. Was it any wonder she resented him for charming her staff so efficiently? Maybe she could more easily forgive him if she wasn't so afraid of falling under his spell herself. Maybe she should be glad he *wasn't* going to perform. She might not survive the excitement. "By the way, do you have any idea why he won't perform himself? I've always wondered…"

"No, I don't." Emma gave a quick slice of her hand to indicate Ana should stop talking, then bobbed her head in the direction of the hall leading toward the back door. "Anyway," she said loudly. "I've got to go. Lots of things to do. Favors to call in and whatnot." She raised her eyebrows in silent question. "We'll talk later?"

Ana pressed her lips together and nodded. Obviously, Ward was coming down the hall. What was it with him sneaking in the back door, anyway?

Emma excused herself just as Ward appeared in her doorway. Ana had hoped she wouldn't have to see him again today. Certainly not alone. Weren't lazy stars supposed to be whiling away the afternoon by the pool or something? For that matter, wasn't he supposed to *be* a lazy star? Why couldn't he just throw a temper tantrum or snort some kelp like she'd expected him to?

"Do you have a minute?" he asked but didn't wait for her answer before entering her office and shutting the door behind him.

"Certainly," she muttered, hoping her tone didn't sound as false to him as it did to her. Her office was little more than a repurposed closet. Between her desk sitting flush against one wall and her bookshelf against the opposite wall, she barely had room for more than her desk chair and the chair she'd set by the door for guests.

He sat down in the extra chair, scooting it back as he did to stretch out his long limbs. She nudged her own chair back a couple of inches to keep from bumping into his legs. His sheer size seemed to swallow up the empty space of her office. Just as the very air seemed permeated by the woodsy scent of his... his what? It wasn't strong or overpowering like a cologne. It was something more subtle. Maybe his soap. Or maybe his skin just naturally smelled like freedom and afternoons spent hiking in the woods. Like—

She gave her head a little shake, trying to free herself from the grasp of her senses. She realized abruptly that he was watching her, his gaze dark and mysterious. She felt awareness skitter across her nerve endings.

She was used to being hit on by men. She had a voluptuous figure and a pretty-enough face. Men often had certain expectations about hot-blooded Latina women and loose morals. Never mind that she'd never once lived down to that stereotype, she was used to having strange men check her out. But this was different.

Ward's stare wasn't leering. He seemed to be assessing her personality rather than her flingability. She feared that if he was sizing her up, he'd find her lacking somehow.

And yet, underneath that, there was a spark of awareness. She'd almost swear to it. Of course, what was more disconcerting was her reaction to him. Why did his mere presence make her feel so much more aware of herself? Of the lock of hair that had slipped free of her clip and sat heavy against her neck. Of the way she'd kicked off her shoes when she'd first sat down and then scooted away from her desk without slipping them back on. Aware of her bare toes, with their silly blue nail polish, mere inches from his expensive leather loafers.

As if sensing her thoughts, he glanced down at her feet. He stared at them long enough to make her uncomfortable. And then swallowed noticeably. She jerked her feet under her chair and curled her toes under. He looked back up at her, his expression carefully blank.

When he spoke, his tone brooked no argument. "We need to talk."

Ah, crap. He *had* been sizing her up. Here it comes. She was unprofessional. She was unqualified. She was disrespectful. He hated blue nail polish and her feet repulsed him.

She felt as though he could see right through her. As though any defense she might make would be fruitless. Not that he gave her a chance to state her case.

"There's one thing I don't tolerate," he stated blandly. "That's people who aren't honest with me. You obviously don't like me and I need to know why."

She didn't…what? She blew out a long breath, trying to process his words. He was worried she didn't like *him?*

"It's not—"

"Either you don't like me or you don't trust me. Something. Let's get it out on the table right now. And don't throw out that crap about not trusting celebrities. Because I don't believe for a second that you'd let that get in the way of making Hannah's Hope a success."

She blew out a deep breath, trying to gauge just how honest she dared to be. Yes, she didn't like celebrities. Ridley Sinclair had made her life horrible and she knew that most male celebrities wouldn't think twice about acting that way. But in all honesty, nothing Ward had done since she'd met him indicated he was anything like those men. Which, somehow, almost made it worse.

She could dismiss someone like Ridley Sinclair. But hardworking, straight-talking Ward? He was much harder to ignore.

Since she couldn't admit any of that aloud, she grasped at straws and pulled the first one that came away in her hand.

"Okay," she said. "For starters, I don't like the way you've stormed in here and taken over. You've been in town less than a day and you're already blowing our budget on whiteboards and catered fruit trays."

"I didn't spend the charity's money on those things."

"Oh." He'd spent his own? She suppressed a groan. Hot and

generous? She was so screwed. Still, he was looking at her expectantly. So she yanked out another straw. "You think that makes it better? That if you throw around money, the things you want will get done?"

He flashed a smile with just a tinge of charming chagrin. "Generally, that is the way it works."

"Well, not in my experience it doesn't. If we're going to reach all of our goals, we need to be realistic and conscientious and—"

"Let's cut to the chase, Ana. Are we going to have a problem working together?" His tone was cold, his gaze quietly assessing.

Alarm bells started jangling in the back of her brain again. She rubbed the sole of one foot across the top of the other. Remember the odds. One superstar. Eighty-nine million bleeding-heart liberals waiting to take her place if she screwed up this job.

But even as that refrain echoed through her brain, she realized it wasn't about that. Not really. The truth was, she didn't really want to be attracted to him. Didn't want to like him.

Ana drew in a deep breath—wishing he wasn't sitting quite so close—and then she exhaled slowly.

Was she going to have a problem working with him? Maybe. Would he ever know it again? No. Nope. *Nada*.

She forced a serene and welcoming smile. "No, Mr. Miller. We won't."

His gaze narrowed slightly at the use of his last name, as if her formality annoyed him. She clenched her hands together to keep herself from fidgeting.

"Did you know, *Ms. Rodriguez,* that I was twelve the first time I performed professionally on stage?"

Disconcerted by his direct stare, she reached her hand up to tuck aside that loose strand of hair. It was all she could do not to fan the back of her neck. "No. I didn't know that."

"I had my first record deal at fifteen. Signed with my first major label at nineteen."

Maybe it was the slow, lazy way he spoke. Or maybe it was the attentive way he met her gaze. This wasn't him bragging. It wasn't him trying to impress her. He was making a point. She had the feeling that when he got there, she wasn't going to like it.

"I've been in this business for twenty-four years. Which is almost as long as you've been alive." He shrugged with a wry smile. "Almost as long as I've been alive, for that matter. In my years in entertainment—" he rocked his chair back onto two legs, steepling his fingers over his chest "—I've dealt with all kinds of people who tried to take advantage of me. I've dealt with people who claimed they wanted to protect me. Wanted to be my best friend. When you're in an industry like this for that long, one of two things happens. Either you become one of those crazy people who snorts kelp up their nose five times a day, or you learn how to tell when someone's lying to you." He let the chair drop forward onto its front legs. "I don't like kelp."

She fought the urge to bite her lip. Dang it, did he have to be funny on top of it all?

"Basically," he continued, "there's only one thing I do better than play guitar and that's know when someone's lying to me. So why don't we start over and you tell me exactly why you have a problem with me."

Three

His blunt honesty knocked the wind out of her. What was she supposed to do with that?

It's not like she could say, "Hey, I think you're really dreamy. Oh, and it kind of pisses me off." Or even worse, "I'm woefully underqualified for this job. I'm barely keeping my head above water here and if you knew how close I was to drowning, you'd get me fired."

Instead, she decided the easiest way to show him where she was coming from was to tell him a story of her own. "I was twelve when my parents moved here from L.A. Even though it's only an hour and a half away, there's a world of difference. My father accepted a job as the Worths' gardener. My mother as their housekeeper. I grew up above the Worths' garage. We may have been the hired help, but they never treated us that way."

He was studying her, elbows propped on his knees, expression intense. Under his gaze, her breath seemed to catch in her chest. It was disconcerting to have him watching her so closely.

She was used to dealing with stars who only cared about your opinion when you were talking about them. But Ward seemed to actually be listening to her. Just like he'd listened to her staff during the brainstorming session.

Suddenly, the room felt tight and small. Like he simply took up too much space. She inched forward to shove her feet back into her shoes, then stood and nodded toward the door. "I'm going to go clean up the conference room. If you want to keep talking, come along. But if we leave that fruit out much longer, it'll go bad."

She knew he'd follow her, of course. It seemed like Ward rarely did what she wished he would. As they walked down the hall, she continued talking.

"I know it sounds like I'm just telling you my life story. But you have to understand, moving here from L.A., it saved my family. Not just my immediate family, but everyone. Once we moved here, aunts and uncles followed."

His gaze narrowed slightly, obviously considering her words, but not yet fully understanding. How could he?

She turned to face him fully. "It may sound cheesy and cliché, but Vista del Mar is a special place. It's not perfect. Sure we have our problems, but we also stick together. And we take care of our own. It was the perfect community to grow up in. To raise a family. At least it used to be. But now that Rafe Cameron has returned and bought Worth Industries…" She let her voice trail off as she realized how that sounded.

Ward must have keyed in on her tone of voice. "Can I assume you don't wholly approve of Rafe?"

She ducked away from his appraising stare and studied the conference room. The detritus of their brainstorming session remained scattered throughout the room. She busied herself first with finding the lid to the fruit tray.

"I don't want to speak badly of him." She positioned the plastic lid in place and snapped it on with precise movements. "He's your friend."

Ward obviously didn't share her sudden need for busyness. Instead, he lowered himself to the conference chair at the head of the table and stretched his legs out in front of him. "He's also your boss."

There was a subtle edge to Ward's voice. A word of warning, perhaps.

Okay. So that's where the line was drawn. Good to know.

She nodded brusquely, ready to turn her attention to the muffin tray. There was only one muffin left. Banana nut chocolate. Her favorite. She left it out on the tray. She might need a healthy dose of chocolate later.

"Don't get me wrong, I certainly appreciate all he's doing with Hannah's Hope."

"Glad you appreciate the millions of dollars he's committed to pouring into the community," Ward said wryly.

Ostensibly, Rafe was head of the board of directors for Hannah's Hope. But as far as she could tell, he wasn't very invested in its success. He'd plopped Ward onto the board to be the face of the charity and then added in Emma, at Ronald Worth's request. Plus, Emma was universally loved. So having her on the board buttered up the local community. Emma, who'd long been involved in other charities, certainly had the experience and the town's goodwill, but Ana couldn't shake the feeling that Rafe had included Emma solely to give the illusion of continuity between the Worth Industries that had been and the new regime to come.

Still, people in town were nervous. People who'd been at Worth Industries for years had been let go or were taking early retirement. Rumor had it, Rafe was bringing in his PR expert, Max Preston. Ana couldn't help feeling suspicious about why a PR expert was needed.

She ignored Ward's subtle dig and continued talking. "Since I've been back, I've noticed the whole feel of the town has changed. People are nervous. Worried. If Rafe closes down the factory, it would be disastrous for Vista del Mar."

"I'm aware of that. But none of that has anything to do with Hannah's Hope."

"Of course it does. I could be more efficient at my job if Rafe were more involved."

Ward frowned, not in an annoyed way, but more as if he was figuring out if he could help. "Involved how?"

"Just more involved." She cleared away the last of the snack plates and grabbed a napkin with which to wipe down the table. "I've met the man precisely once and only for a handful of minutes when Emma brought me down for my official interview." She resisted making air quotes around the word *interview,* but was unable to keep the disdain from her voice. Instead, she swiped the last of the crumbs into her waiting palm.

Her entire interview had consisted of waiting for over an hour, only to be led into his office, have him give her the once-over and return his attention to the laptop open in front of him. "Emma thinks you'll do a good job. Don't disappoint her."

That had been the entire interview.

She dusted the crumbs off her palm and into the trash. There. That was better.

"You should be careful what you wish for," Ward chided her. "Rafe can be an extremely demanding boss."

She looked up to find him studying her with that intensity she found so unnerving. Funny, she'd thought it was the proximity that made him so nerve-racking. But it turned out he was disconcerting no matter how big the room.

"True though that may be, I would still appreciate a smidge more involvement from him." She crossed to the chairs where the whiteboards were still propped. An eraser sat on one of the chair cushions, still in its plastic wrapper. "Other than the one time we've met, he's only communicated via email. Every time I've sent him a question, he's responded the same way." She ripped the plastic off the eraser as she lowered her voice to mimic the way she imagined Rafe would sound if he were to take the time to actually pick up the phone and call her. "'I trust your judgment.' That's all he says." She rubbed the eraser across the slick surface of the whiteboard. It was oddly satisfying to strip away the evidence of the brainstorming session. If only all of her problems were that easily dealt with. "I've started to think he's just copying and pasting from previous emails."

"Or, he trusts Emma's recommendation."

While she'd been busy taking out her frustration on the whiteboard, Ward had stood and crossed to her side. She glanced up to find him standing far too close. Close enough for her to see the tiny flecks of gold in his eyes. How had he moved so silently?

She sucked in a deep breath and was once again struck by the scent of him. So clean and crisp. When she spoke, her words came out almost as a whisper. "He barely knows Emma."

She cleared her throat, annoyed with herself for being distracted. Ward's gold-flecked eyes were the least of her worries. But…what were her worries again?

Right. The fact that Rafe didn't know Emma well enough to trust her opinion. And he knew Ana even less well. Given her scanty qualifications, how could she view Rafe's trust as anything other than negligence?

"But he's known Chase for years. If his brother trusts Emma, then Rafe does, too." Ward reached out a hand to her arm.

Obviously, he meant it to comfort her, but instead it sent tiny fissures of awareness coursing through her. And then she looked down at it. His hand was large. Strong and powerful. His fingertips rough against her skin. And just so…capable.

Her breath rushed out of her lungs. It hit her then. This wasn't just the strong and masculine hand of an attractive man. This was Ward Miller's hand. The hand he used to do all that fret work for which his songs were so famous.

Something giddy and girlish stirred within her. Something deeply feminine. She felt her breath coming in short bursts as warmth flowed over her.

She forced her gaze from that spot on her arm where his skin touched hers, only to find herself looking up into his eyes, again. Dang it. Those were some dangerous eyes. They were eyes she could lose herself in.

Which was *so* not good, seeing as how lost she already felt.

She shook her head to clear it and tried to remember what she'd been saying. Hannah's Hope. Right. How overwhelmed she felt. "I just…could use a little guidance. More involvement. More hands-on."

"Well, then. You're going to love me," he murmured.

Then her gaze darted once again to where his hand still rested on her arm. Why hadn't he moved it yet? Why hadn't she simply stepped away? She felt heat flood her cheeks and she jerked her arm away.

She forced a stern note into her voice. "This isn't a joke. Hannah's Hope is important. It's not just a charity, it's an opportunity to bring together the whole community."

"I knew that already," he said, his own tone devoid of charm or humor. "Rafe convinced me of that before I even came out here. You're right about one thing." He gently pried the eraser from her hand and began cleaning the second whiteboard. "You can't depend on Rafe."

She forced her attention away from the smooth confident movement of his hands, surprised at his bluntness. "But—"

"He'll do right by Hannah's Hope. I guarantee that. But it would be shortsighted of you to rely solely on him for financing. You need to get more money flowing in and you need to get the word out about what you're doing. That's what I'm here to help with."

His voice had that low seductive quality again that beckoned to her. Made her all too aware of how vulnerable she felt. And made her wish she had more crumbs to clean up.

Thankfully, he seemed unaware of it as he continued, "The Cara Miller Foundation has a lot of good people working for it. If you don't trust me or Rafe, then at least trust them to do their job."

She clenched and unclenched her hands in front of her, hating how nauseated she felt at hearing her own concerns voiced aloud. "So you think bringing someone in from CMF to do my job would be better for Hannah's Hope?"

"Whoa—" He held up his hands in the universal sign of surrender. "That's not even close to what I said."

"But you do think someone else could do a better job?" Resentment spiked through her. Who was he to criticize the way they were doing things? He was a musician. It's not like he had any hands-on experience running a nonprofit…okay, so he did have hands-on experience. "I'm sure that when you started the Cara Miller Foundation, you hired all the best people in the industry and were able to get things up and running in nothing flat."

She tried to keep the bitterness from her voice. The Cara Miller Foundation was known all over the world for its work in early childhood healthcare. But she had no doubt that part of what had made the Cara Miller Foundation so successful was Ward. He'd brought the full force of his personality—not to mention his considerable wealth—to bear in the charity.

She released a deep breath, determined not to take out her frustration on Ward. Even if he was friends with Rafe, it wasn't his fault that Hannah's Hope was little more than an afterthought to Cameron Enterprises' purchase of Worth Industries.

She paced to the far side of the conference room, but even that far away from him, she felt like his nearness was smothering her.

"You have to see where I'm coming from. The Cara Miller Foundation is a study in efficiency and effectiveness. The work you've done is..." She shrugged, looking for the perfect word. "Legendary."

His lips curved in a faint smile, graciously acknowledging her compliment. "Thanks. CMF has a lot of great people working for it."

"Exactly," she agreed grimly. "And Hannah's Hope has me."

"That's not what I meant." He shook his head ruefully.

"I'm not one to pull my punches. Especially not when I'm dealing with my own failings." She sighed, scraping her hair off her face, even though only a few locks had escaped. "I desperately wanted this job. And I desperately wanted to be great at it. And I'm just..." She floundered, finding it harder than she imagined it would be to put her own shortcomings into words. "I'm not as good at this as I expected. I thought the volunteer work I'd done in L.A. would be a solid groundwork for this. Plus, I'm smart. I'm hardworking, I've never failed at anything in my life. I thought that would be enough. But so far, it's not. The sheer minutia associated with setting up a nonprofit is completely overwhelming me."

As soon as the words left her mouth, she snapped her mouth closed, wishing she could take them back. Jeez, of all the people to gripe to… Why'd she pick one of the two people who could summarily fire her? The board held her job in their hands. Emma would never vote to fire her, but if Ward persuaded Rafe, they'd have the majority.

But when she met his gaze, there was more understanding there than censure. His lips were twisted in a wry smile. His eyebrows lifted slightly.

"Don't get me wrong. I'm not afraid of hard work. I'm not even afraid of failing. I just don't want to disappoint others. In the four years I worked in Hollywood, I dealt with some of the most difficult personalities in the industry. After that, I was so sure I could handle anything." Now she did laugh as she admitted, "God, I hate being wrong."

He walked to where she was, then gently turned her to face him. "You weren't wrong. You can do this."

The fervor in his eyes, the sheer conviction nearly took her breath away. She was struck all over again by how handsome he was. By the fact that Ward Miller—Ward Freakin' Miller—was here, mere inches away from her. Talking to her like a colleague. She shook it off. This was so not the time to wallow in his intense sexual appeal.

Abruptly, he dropped his hands and shoved them into his back pockets. "I remember all too well how hard it was to get CMF started. Sure, I had staff. I had hired the best people in the business, but I wanted to do most of it myself. I needed something to keep me busy."

She found herself practically holding her breath. It had been three years since his wife had died. Still, she didn't imagine that was something you ever got over.

She'd looked him up on Google when Emma first called to tell her he was the third board member. After carefully tucking all her girlish fantasies back away, she'd realized that she knew very little about what he'd been doing in life since he'd disappeared from the public eye.

The web had enough details about Cara's death to satisfy the most morbidly curious, up to and including Ward's last words to her.

She'd been so disgusted by the invasion of his privacy that she'd immediately closed the window, feeling a bit unsavory for reading even as much as she had. Losing a loved one was hard enough, but to have your grief splattered all over the tabloids for public consumption, that was…well, just unimaginable.

"It must have been extremely hard to lose her," she said now.

He nodded, his expression patient, somehow accepting of her awkward, fumbling condolences. "If I could start CMF," he continued, "then so can you. That's why I'm here to help."

But she shook her head. "It's enough that you're on the board, that you're being the face of Hannah's Hope. I'm certainly not going to ask you to do my job on top of that."

"I'm not doing your job," he argued. "I'm doing *my* job."

"I don't understand."

He smiled at her obvious confusion. "You don't know what CMF does, do you?"

"It provides healthcare for impoverished children."

"That's half of what the Cara Miller Foundation does." His grin lit with mischief. Like he was about to share a secret. She felt herself leaning toward him. "When I started CMF, that was my intent. But along the way I realized how hard it was to start a nonprofit. I quickly realized that without the financial and personal resources I had, I never would have gotten anywhere. That's why I started the other branch of CMF."

She frowned. "The other branch?"

"Yes. Helping kids was Cara's thing. But that's not what really excites me."

"What is?" Heat flooded her cheeks as she realized the double meaning behind her question. But she quickly forced her embarrassment aside. Yes, there seemed to be an attraction simmering between them, but he seemed determined to ignore it. And if he could, then she certainly could, too.

She forced her attention to the topic at hand. She'd thought she knew exactly what the Cara Miller Foundation did. She'd thought she knew exactly why he was here. Just to provide a glamorous face to promote Hannah's Hope. Had she been wrong?

"I've lost you, haven't I?"

"A little bit," she admitted, chagrined because he seemed to read her as easily as if she had thought bubbles dangling over her head.

"Let me back up. Have you ever heard the term *business incubator?*"

"I think so." She'd read an article in the paper not too long ago about them. "They're companies whose sole purpose is to help new companies get started, right?"

"Exactly. The secondary branch of the Cara Miller Foundation—the branch that doesn't get a lot of publicity and isn't in the news all the time—is a nonprofit incubator. We find people with great intentions and dedicated personnel and we help them get their nonprofit off the ground. We don't do the work for people, we just provide them with the training and resources they need to get the job done."

"I had no idea such a thing even existed." Surprise—no, to be honest it was out-and-out shock—washed over her. "How did I not know this?"

"I don't know." For a second he looked as baffled as she felt. Then he quickly shrugged it off. "Rafe certainly knew. It's why he asked me to be on the board."

"Yes, and he's been such a font of information," she muttered drily. "If that's why you're here, I should have been told that before you showed up." Her indignation crept into her voice. She didn't like being kept out of the loop.

"I thought you were."

"Well, I wasn't and—" But she broke off, frowning as she tried to summon up exactly how the conversation had gone the night Emma had called with the information about Ward coming.

What had Emma said about Ward? Had she even really listened to Emma's explanation? There'd probably been a solid thirty seconds during which Ana had dropped the phone and silently squealed in excitement.

And then, a few minutes later, it had really hit her. Ward Miller. Working with her. But working *for* Rafe.

Her excitement had given way to unease. All of her real-life knowledge of celebrities had slammed head-on into her fandom. To do her job, she'd have to bury her fantasies. To protect Hannah's Hope, she'd have to be suspicious of his every action. She'd have to set aside everything she wanted to believe about him.

Throughout that epiphany, Emma had kept on talking, possibly explaining exactly everything Ward was bringing to the table. And Ana's cynicism had made her miss it.

Now, she cringed. "It's possible that Emma explained everything and I just didn't hear her." She sighed, massaging the tension in her forehead with her fingers. "That must be what happened. Emma wouldn't have purposefully left it out."

Emma put her heart and soul into her charity work. Which was why making sure Hannah's Hope flourished was so important. Ana couldn't bear to let Emma down. And knowing what she knew now, she didn't want to let Ward down, either. If he wasn't going to immediately kick her sorry butt to the curb, if he was going to give her another chance, she was going to grab it with both hands and never let it go.

Full of renewed resolve, she straightened. "Okay, Mr. Nonprofit Incubator, you're the expert. Where do we go from here?"

Four

Ana's question hung in the air between them. Where do we go from here?

He could think of about a dozen places they could go. Dinner. Some cozy restaurant where he could ply her with food and wine. Down to the beach where he could coax her into kicking off her shoes to walk with him on the sand. Where he could free her hair from that maddening knot she'd worn it in and bury his nose in the skin at the nape of her neck. Breathe in that intoxicating cinnamon scent.

Hey, he had a lot of suggestions. None of them were the least bit appropriate. Not for a woman he worked with.

So he buried his gut-level reaction and gave her the answer she really needed. "We go to Charleston."

She blinked in surprise. "Come again?"

Ward nearly laughed at the sheer disbelief on Ana's face. "Charleston," he repeated.

"The city?"

"Yes, the city. I certainly wasn't planning on taking you

dancing." A look of confusion flickered across her face and he added, "I have horrible rhythm."

She narrowed her gaze, clearly unsure how to take his words. "Somehow I doubt that."

"Honest to God. I can't dance to save my life."

She just shook her head, obviously deciding to ignore his teasing. "What's in Charleston?"

"The Cara Miller Foundation headquarters. Once you see the kinds of things we do there—"

She didn't let him finish but cut him off. "Are you insane?"

Again, she didn't give him a chance to answer, and he let her talk, her impassioned words pouring out in a stream. "I admit that the street fair is a good idea, but between that and my normal work, I can't possibly jaunt off to Charleston on a whim. Even if we had the money in our budget for such a trip—which we don't—I can't take the time away from work."

Frankly, it impressed the hell out of him that she had the confidence to rant at him. Most people didn't. She seemed to have the unique ability to forget that he was a superstar.

"This isn't time away from work," he pointed out. "I'm not suggesting you come to Charleston to go sightseeing. It'll be a working trip. You can meet our lawyers and accountants. People who can make the work you're struggling with here go twice as fast. Two, three days max. If we leave Sunday night I'll have you back in San Diego in plenty of time to get ready for Chase and Emma's wedding next weekend."

She seemed to consider it for a moment. Then firmly shook her head. "I just don't see how I could justify—"

He took that as a yes. She kept on talking as he pulled out his iPhone and dialed his assistant. He was midway through the conversation before she even noticed he wasn't listening. She came to stand directly in front of him, hands propped on her hips, gaze narrowed in annoyance.

"Hang on, Jess," he said into the phone before he lowered it. He cocked an eyebrow at her in silent question.

"Did I just hear you say 'first class'?"

"It's a long flight. At night. You really don't want to fly coach."

"*I* don't want?" she repeated. "*I* don't want to go at all."

"I know that. But you're going to have to trust me. The trip will be worth it."

Before he could explain more, Jess started talking again and Ward turned his attention to him. He was listening to Jess's reply as he felt a tap-tap-tap on his biceps. He glanced over to see Ana frowning at him, arms crossed over her chest.

Into the phone he said, "Call me back with the details on the flight. Thanks."

As he slipped the phone back into his front shirt pocket, her scowl deepened.

"I can't just run off to Charleston for the weekend."

"Of course you can."

"No. I can't. In addition to all the paperwork—which I'm ridiculously behind on—" she gestured to the whiteboard behind her "—now I also have to plan a street fair."

He laughed outright. "You've already said all of this. Now you're just grasping at straws. Besides, you don't have to do anything about the street fair."

"Of course I do." She threw her hands up in the air in obvious frustration. "Everyone here is excited about it and—"

He gently grabbed her arms. "Exactly. *They're* excited about it. Let them handle it. You don't have to be in charge of everything. Jess could do this kind of thing in his sleep. Presumably, your people have contacts here who can smooth the way. My PR guy, Ryan, is relatively new and still eager to prove he's useful. Frankly, I haven't had a lot for him to do yet. He'll be thrilled to have something to keep him busy."

"You make it sound so easy." Her tone was heavy with accusation.

"It is easy," he assured her.

For an instant, doubt flickered across her face. He was struck by how warm and solid her arms felt under his hands. Unlike so many of the women he knew in show business, Ana had meat on her bones. She certainly wasn't overweight, but she wasn't scrawny, either. Her arms were leanly muscled, her body curvy in all the right places. This was a hell of a time for him to notice it.

Suddenly, he was all too aware of her very feminine body only a foot away from his. He sucked in a deep breath, trying to quell the urge to pull her fully into his arms. Unfortunately, that only drew in the scent of her. That warm cinnamon-vanilla smell that called to him so strongly. Again, an image of her flashed through his mind. Her hair loose about her shoulders, her neck arched back, exposing the long column of her throat to his lips.

Abruptly, he released his hold on her and stepped away.

Bringing her to CMF's headquarters was the right thing to do. She needed the knowledge CMF could give her. And Hannah's Hope needed her as well-educated as possible.

But bringing her to Charleston was the last thing he needed. He was too damned attracted to her already. Spending time with her would only make that worse. But what was he supposed to do? Walk away from someone who needed this help merely because he was having trouble keeping his zipper up?

Besides which, he'd told Rafe that he'd help. He kept his promises. And he would keep this one, even if it damn near killed him. He just wished he didn't have to fight her as well as his own instincts.

He turned back to her, forcing a smile. "I'll make you a deal. You come to Charleston with me and spend three days at CMF. When you get back, if you're not convinced it was the right thing to do, I'll personally donate enough money to cover whatever the street fair costs."

She narrowed her gaze in suspicion. "I can't let you pay for that."

Of course she couldn't. She'd bristled at forty bucks worth of muffins and coffee.

He quirked an eyebrow knowing it would irritate her. "You don't think I'm good for it?"

"No."

He couldn't resist purposefully misunderstanding her. "I have plenty of money."

"Obviously," she scoffed. "That's not what I meant. I can't let you just give us the money."

"It's a donation."

"It's not a donation," she countered. "It's a bribe."

He slung an arm around her shoulder, like a good buddy. The gesture backfired. Once again, the scent of her hit him. Beneath his hand, her shoulder felt both delicate and strong. Her posture was stiff and unyielding, like she didn't quite trust his intentions. Smart lady.

'Cause yeah, he was just a good buddy. A good buddy who got rock-hard every time he caught a whiff of her hair. A good buddy who wanted to strip away all her layers of professional clothing to see the naked body beneath. Hell, who wanted to strip away all her emotional defenses and see what was beneath those, too.

Yeah, that was just the kind of buddy she needed.

Nevertheless, like a good buddy, he gently guided her toward the table where one lone muffin still sat. He'd seen her eyeing the muffin earlier. "First rule of nonprofit—when an insanely rich donor wants to give you money, you accept it."

"That's not…" she sputtered. "I didn't…" She threw up her hands in frustration. "You're twisting my words."

"I don't think it's your words I'm twisting." He pressed a muffin into her hand.

She took a bite, despite the scowl on her face. She looked exactly like a recalcitrant toddler miffed at being talked into going to bed early on Christmas Eve. "Has anyone ever told you you're a very difficult man to deal with?"

He grinned. "Second rule of nonprofits—don't insult the insanely rich donors giving you money."

She gave him a tight smile. "That wasn't an insult. It was a question." She broke off another bite of muffin and popped it into her mouth. Her voice dripped with mock enthusiasm when she asked, "Are there any other rules of nonprofits I need to know?"

"We'll go over them on the plane."

He still wasn't sure how exactly he was supposed to spend a

five-and-a-half-hour flight with her. He sure as hell wasn't going to be able to sleep with her in the seat beside him.

The good news was, she didn't look any more enthusiastic about it than he felt.

She forced a smile. "Yippee."

After Ward's comments Friday, Ana had fully expected him to make the trip with her. When he wasn't in the car that came to pick her up, she assumed he'd meet her at the terminal. But he hadn't shown up there, either. He'd sent Jess to explain that Rafe had rescheduled the board meeting for the following morning. When she'd offered to stay for the meeting herself, Jess quickly assured her that wasn't necessary. Instead, she was hustled onto the plane, leaving her with the feeling that she was being "handled."

Thirty-six hours later, at least one of her fears had been alleviated. She didn't yet know if Ward doubted her abilities, but it was obvious from her treatment at CMF that he wasn't angling to get her fired. Surely if he had been, the CMF employees wouldn't have rolled out the carpet for her on such a grand scale.

Once the plane had landed in Charleston, she'd been whisked off to the hotel to freshen up and rest. Luckily, she'd been able to sleep on the plane and needed only a brief nap before her whirlwind tour of CMF. She'd spent a few hours shadowing the director of the charitable branch of CMF. The woman, Stacy Goebel, had been a friend of Cara's and had been an executive at a marketing firm before Ward had offered her the job. That evening, Stacy had taken Ana to dinner at a local landmark before dropping her off at the hotel. The next day was more of the same, except at the incubator branch of the charity.

By noon, her mind was reeling from how much she'd learned. Things she hadn't even thought she needed to know. Stacy had scheduled a lunch with CMF's on-staff lawyer, who was able to recommend a lawyer in San Diego that could work with Hannah's Hope. Then it was back to CMF for the afternoon. By the time they ended for the day, Ana could hardly think straight.

Once again, Stacy had planned to take her out to dinner. Waiting for Stacy in the front lobby, Ana occupied herself by gawking. Until now, she'd been carted from meeting to meeting at such a brisk pace that she hadn't had much of a chance to look around. Now that she did, she felt another burst of giddy, fan-girl excitement.

CMF's lobby was decorated with trophies from Ward's music career. The main reception desk sat in the middle of the room, a small waiting area was off to the side. Gold and platinum albums covered so much of the wall that it almost looked like wallpaper.

Stacy made it into the lobby just about the time Ana had reached the back wall where a beat-up Alvarez Yairi acoustic guitar sat on a stand encased in glass. Its burled mahogany back and sides gleamed a rich brown under the lights. The solid cedar front was worn and scuffed.

"Ah, I see you found the gallery."

"It's an impressive collection." It was a fitting tribute to Ward's extraordinary career. "It seems…I don't know. Out of place, maybe. Ward doesn't seem the type to be quite so ostentatious."

"He's not," Stacy quickly defended her boss.

Ana hid her cringe. "I didn't mean that the way it sounded."

"No, honestly. Ward doesn't like this room at all. The decorator suggested it. Ward's never comfortable here, but even he admits that it's a hit whenever we host fundraisers here. Donors love it."

Ana nodded. That did seem like Ward. Willing to flaunt his fame only when it got him what he wanted. In this case, money for CMF.

"What do you think?" Stacy asked when she saw Ana staring at the guitar.

"That's not *the* Alvarez, is it?"

Stacy grinned gleefully as if she could fully appreciate the reverence in Ana's voice. "It is. The Alvarez."

There was a certain breed of rock star that delighted in destroying expensive guitars. They abused them as a sign of their decadence. Ward had never been that kind of musician. He'd been playing music on the same beat-up Alvarez guitar he bought used from a store in Memphis when he was fifteen. One of the many bits of trivia any fan would know. The guitar had become legendary. As much a part of his mystique as his gravelly voice and trademark fretwork.

Standing beside her, Stacy sighed. "You know, Cara and I had been best friends for years when she started dating Ward. I was completely in awe when I met him. The first time I saw this guitar—" she rolled her eyes as if amused by her own silliness "—I couldn't stop staring at it. I cried the first time I heard him play it in person."

Ana could certainly understand that. Her fingers practically twitched with the urge to touch it. They probably kept it behind glass to keep greedy fan fingers off it.

"What's in its place when the Alvarez isn't here?" she asked.

Stacy shrugged, sorrow crossing her face. "The Alvarez is always here."

"How is that possible? From what I've read, that's the only guitar he composes on. That's *his* guitar."

She broke off, suddenly aware of how obsessive she sounded.

Stacy seemed not to notice. "We opened our doors about four months after Cara died. As far as I know, the only people who ever touch it are the nightly cleaning crew."

"He never…" Ana prodded.

"No," Stacy answered the unasked question. "He never does."

Her throat closed over her emotions. "That makes me very sad," Ana admitted.

Stacy smiled ruefully. "Me, too."

Ward kept his career and his talent behind carefully constructed glass, away from the dust, away from most eyes and away from any touch, especially his own.

Shaking off the sad mood, Stacy turned toward Ana and smiled. "So, did you decide the trip was worth it after all?"

Ana shot the other woman a surprised look. "Excuse me?"

Stacy smiled slyly. "When you first showed up, you seemed… hesitant. Or maybe suspicious."

Ana had to smile in return. "I guess I'm not as good at hiding my feelings as I thought." She brushed aside a lock of hair that had fallen loose from the twist, and tucked it behind her ear. "Suspicious about sums it up. I'd been floundering a bit at Hannah's Hope. I honestly didn't believe coming all the way out here would help when there was so much work to be done back home." And then she laughed at her own foolishness. "And I thought maybe Ward was just trying to get me out of the way so he could call a board meeting without me."

Stacy shot her a confused look. "Why would he do that?"

Ana forced a rueful smile. "You're going to think I'm being overly paranoid, but I'm not sure how to read Ward. I figured, if he thought I was doing a crappy job at Hannah's Hope, he might decide it was just easier to get me out of the way and hire someone better qualified."

She adjusted her purse strap on her shoulder as they headed out of the lobby for the parking garage.

Stacy was quiet for a long moment and when Ana glanced over at her, it was to see the other woman frowning.

Stacy noticed and smiled brightly. "Well, at least I can put that concern to rest. He never would have flown you out here if he didn't plan on keeping you at Hannah's Hope for a long time."

"Really? Isn't this what CMF does all the time?"

"Yes and no." Stacy bobbled her head from side to side to indicate her ambivalence. "Yes, we help other nonprofits. That's one of our primary missions, but usually we do most of our work virtually, using videoconferencing and online classes. We consult via email and phone calls. Of course, all those resources will be available to you as well, but Ward arranged this for you as a sort of…crash course." Stacy must have seen the consternation flicker across her face, because she rushed to reassure her. "Not because he doesn't think you're capable, but because he's so enthusiastic about the work Hannah's Hope is doing. In fact, when I saw him this morning he—"

"Wait a second," Ana interrupted her. "You saw Ward this morning?"

"He was here early this morning and then left just before you arrived."

"I see," she muttered. Except she really didn't. Her first meeting at CMF had been scheduled at nine. He'd have had to have come in at seven or seven-thirty to get in a meeting and leave before she even got there. "Is that normal for him? Scheduling meetings that early?"

"Thank goodness, no." Stacy stifled a yawn. "Normally, he comes into the office about nine."

"He must have had a busy day scheduled to make you come in so early."

But Stacy shook her head. "No, that's the weird thing. Jess always sends his schedule on to me when he's in town. He didn't have anything to do today. Normally, when he's in town, he's here at the office for twelve-hour days. I don't know what's up with this visit that he's staying away. I mean—"

But then Stacy broke off abruptly, giving Ana an odd look. She tilted her head to the side as if Ana were an object of extreme curiosity.

"What?" Ana asked.

Stacy's cheeks flushed red and she averted her gaze. "Nothing," she insisted with sudden cheer. She clapped her hands together. "So, what sounds good for dinner? There's a new Asian fusion restaurant that's been getting great reviews. Or if you want something less formal, there's a great burger joint just down the road. Or—"

"You know, I think I'll skip it tonight." Ana yawned, thankful she didn't have to fake her exhaustion. "It's been a busy few days. I think I'll just head back to the hotel and make an early night of it."

Stacy studied her, her keen gaze assessing. "Are you sure?"

"Positive. Besides, I've got to be here first thing in the morning. I want to squeeze in a little more work before the flight out tomorrow afternoon."

Stacy looked doubtful. Like she'd had very strict orders to

keep an eye on Ana and was afraid that letting her eat alone
would offend the powers that be.

"And you've had a long day yourself," Ana added persuasively.
"You deserve the evening off. I'll be fine on my own. I'll stay
out of trouble. I promise."

She smiled gamely, trying to inject her face with just enough
fatigue to make her claims of exhaustion believable.

Stacy nodded, despite still looking doubtful. "Sure. Fine. Do
you need directions back to the hotel or anything?"

"Nope. The rental came with GPS. I can get wherever I need
to go."

Which was useful, because she wasn't actually heading back
to the hotel. Nope, she was going to track down Ward Miller.
It was time they had a nice long talk. Apparently, during those
conversations they'd had about whether she had a problem with
him, she should have been asking a few questions of her own.

Five

A few minutes later, she steered her car out of CMF's parking lot, aware of Stacy's car not far behind her. But as soon as Stacy's car turned to get on the highway, Ana steered her own car into the parking lot of a nearby strip mall. Once she killed the engine, she pulled out her cell phone. She tried Ward's number first, then left a message when it rolled over to voice mail. Since she didn't hold out high hopes that he would call her back, next she dialed Emma's number.

"Okay," she grumbled, after they got the normal greetings out of the way. "What's the deal with Ward?"

Emma let out a bark of laughter. "What do you mean?"

"I know he's supposed to be one of Chase's best friends, but I've got to say he's being very difficult to work with."

"What's he doing? I mean, I know he has that artistic temperament argument to fall back on, but Chase swears he's a perfectly sane, normal person."

"Hmm," Ana grunted thoughtfully. "So then it really is just me."

"Just you what?"

"Just me that he doesn't like."

"No. I'm sure you're imagining it."

"I'm not," she insisted. "Stacy, the director of CMF, said he normally comes in to work every day he's in town, but he's been avoiding the office since I've been there. I can understand him not coming out on the same flight, because of the board meeting yesterday, but—"

Emma interrupted her. "There wasn't a board meeting yesterday."

"There wasn't? Because Jess said that was why he didn't fly out when I did. That Rafe had rescheduled a board meeting for the morning."

"Oh," Emma said blankly. Even she had run out of arguments.

"Look, I want to talk to him. Apparently, he's avoiding me like I'm some sort of crazed member of the paparazzi." She'd almost said like a crazed fan, but that might be a little too close to the truth. "Can you ask Chase for his address?"

"I'll see what I can do," Emma said with a sigh.

Ten minutes later, Ana typed a new address into the rental's GPS. Following the gadget's directions, she headed deeper into Charleston, to a neighborhood dotted with old houses and even older churches. The tourist map from the rental agency described the neighborhood as Harleston Village. All of the houses on the block had been painstakingly restored and maintained, like well-loved family heirlooms. The multistory homes were nestled close together with only the width of the driveway separating the various buildings. Ward's house sat in the middle of the block with nothing to distinguish it. If she hadn't gotten the address from Emma, she would never have guessed it was the home of a rock star.

She parked her car on the street, wedging it in the narrow space between two of the driveways. The house was right on the street and after quickly mustering her courage, she left the car and went up the steps to the front door. She gave the knocker a quick bang, then waited, her heart pounding in her chest.

A long moment passed during which she wondered if she was

making a huge mistake. After all, what did it really matter if Ward didn't like her? If he wanted to go to great lengths to avoid her, why should she let that bother her? After all, rule number three of nonprofits was probably "if a billionaire donor wanted to act like a reclusive nutcase, let him."

But before she could change her mind, the front door swung open. Instead of Ward, Ana found herself facing a thin middle-aged woman with a pinched, severe expression.

The woman scowled at her and pointed to a sign by the door. "No solicitation," she grumbled, as if Ana couldn't read.

"I'm looking for Ward Miller," Ana explained.

The woman's expression tightened. Then she schooled her features into strained blankness. "Who?"

"This is his house, isn't it?" Ana asked.

"No solicitation," the woman repeated, starting to shut the door.

Ana wedged her foot in the door, wincing as it slammed into her foot. "I got his address from Chase Larson."

The pressure on her foot eased up a little, but the suspicion didn't leave the woman's gaze. "So?"

"I'm Ana Rodriguez. I've been working with Ward and CMF for a charity called Hannah's Hope out near San Diego. He's on the board." The shrew seemed to be wavering, so Ana added, "I only need to talk to him for a few minutes. Why don't you ask him if he'll see me?"

"He's not here," the woman said reluctantly.

"But this is his house, isn't it?"

The woman's gaze narrowed, but finally she nodded.

"Can you tell me when you expect him back?"

"That's easy," the woman said with a faint sneer. "He's not coming back."

"What?" The woman's smug tone grated on Ana's nerves. She narrowed her gaze and edged her shoulders through the gap in the door, refusing to be bullied. It took more to intimidate her than a mere disapproving scowl. "Look, I know he's in town. So you might as well tell him I'm here."

The woman seemed to waffle, then released her hold on the

door so it swung open. Ana grabbed the chance while it was there and slipped through the front door.

The house was as lovely on the inside as it was on the outside. The foyer opened to a living area on one side and a dining room on the other. Directly in front of the door, stairs led up to the second floor. Dark hardwood floors gleamed underfoot. The walls were painted a rich cream that complemented the pristine ivory upholstery. All of which was the perfect backdrop for the stunning collection of abstract art that graced the walls. She tried not to gape. And she definitely didn't ask about them. She didn't really want to know if that was an original Kline. And she really, really didn't want to know if that was a Pollock.

But she supposed this was what she got by invading the home of an icon.

There was only one thing in the foyer more shocking than the millions of dollars worth of art. Sitting on the console right beside the front door, nestled beside a three-foot-tall, orange glass vase, sat a pair of oversize Burberry sunglasses. Exactly like the ones Cara Miller had been famous for wearing.

As if Cara Miller had walked through the front door a few minutes earlier and dropped them there on her way past.

Ana looked from the sunglasses to the disapproving house-keeper, who returned her gaze with a steely obstinacy. Even if Ana hadn't seen countless photos of Cara in similar sunglasses, she could have guessed to whom these belonged.

In general, housekeepers didn't leave their sunglasses on the console by the door. And this was not the sort of woman to wear a two-hundred-dollar accessory.

The sight of those sunglasses sent a fissure of unease skirting down her spine. She shouldn't have seen them. There was some-thing far too intimate about seeing Cara Miller's glasses. They were such tangible proof of Ward's grief. She had invaded his privacy as clearly as if she'd walked in on him half-naked.

She shouldn't have come here.

But damn it, this was his fault, too. If he'd taken her call earlier, she *wouldn't* have come. If he'd had the common decency to talk to her and explain what she'd done to irritate him, then this all could have been avoided.

She swept her gaze around the rooms once again, searching for any signs Ward might be there. She found none. The house was meticulously maintained, but there was a sterility about it. Other than the sunglasses, there were no signs that anyone might have been here in the past year, let alone the past few hours. There were no keys by the door. No half-opened mail. No dog-eared novel on the table beside the sofa. All the furniture sat at precise right angles.

Propping her hands on her hips, she turned back to the house-keeper. "I suppose you were telling the truth. Ward really isn't here."

The housekeeper shook her head and something sad flickered across her face. "He doesn't stay at the house anymore when he comes to town."

As the woman spoke, her gaze darted to the glasses by the door. It was enough. Ana could read between the lines. Ward may still own this house, but he hadn't lived here since Cara died.

Ana nodded. "If you talk to him, ask him to call me."

She'd climbed back into her car already and was backing up, when she happened to glance down the driveway that ran alongside the house. In the back, set away from the house, was a two-story garage. She would guess at some point in the house's long history, it had been a carriage house. Now, it was a garage with an apartment above it.

"He doesn't stay at the *house*," Ana repeated the housekeeper's words. Not, he doesn't stay *here*. But he doesn't stay *at the house*.

On a hunch, Ana turned her car into the driveway and drove past the house. She parked her car in front of the broad carriage house doors and climbed out. A flight of stairs led up the outside of the building to a second-story door. She knew instantly her instincts had been right. She paused at the top of the stairs before knocking. Music drifted through the closed door. She recognized the sultry guitar of blues musician Keb Mo, an artist she started

listening to after reading an interview in which Ward listed Keb
Mo as being on his current playlist.

She knocked. And then after a minute, knocked more loudly
to be heard over the music. A second later, she heard a phone
ringing and then the music was turned down. When Ward opened
the door, he still held his phone in his hand. But she barely
noticed that. Because he was shirtless.

His chest was lightly sprinkled with hair, his skin tanned and
lean. Not bulky or over-muscled. Just… She blew out a breath.
Just…yummy. There was no other word for it.

She knew plenty of men who waxed their chests. She'd lived
in L.A., where every man strove to look like a Ken doll. Men
took such pride in those perfectly smooth, almost boyish chests,
seemingly unaware of how emasculated they looked.

There was nothing emasculated about Ward. Not. A single.
Thing.

For the first time in her life, she understood the feeling other
women had described of itching to touch a man's chest.

Her fingers practically twitched with the urge to touch and
explore. To taste. To lick. To…

Oh, crap. Was she drooling?

She clenched her hands tightly in front of her, choking back
her more primitive urges.

Unfortunately—or fortunately, depending on how she looked
at it—Ward pulled a sweater over his head and tugged it down,
removing temptation. He gave a quick rub to his hair. Only then
did she realize it was damp. Which explained why he'd been
shirtless. Not that she'd been complaining.

"Don't worry about it," he said into the phone just before
ending the call. He shot an exasperated look at her. "That was
my housekeeper warning me you were here."

He stepped aside to let her in. At least he had the good grace
to look chagrined. As if he half expected her to give him a hard
time for having his housekeeper give her the rigmarole.

But she figured she had enough to give him hell about without
bringing that to the table. So instead she stayed quiet for a
moment, taking stock of her surroundings.

From the outside, the carriage house was designed in the same style as the original house. Inside, however, they were completely different. The main house had been bright and well lit with a decor so crisp it bordered on institutional. As far as she could tell, the apartment consisted of a small living area and a tiny kitchenette. A hallway led to what she assumed was a bedroom and bath. A take-out box sat open on the kitchen counter, a bottle of Gran Patron Platinum and a tumbler next to it.

The furniture in the apartment was worn and a little shabby. The woods all exotic dark woods, the upholstery chocolate-brown and warm red batiks. Shelves lined the back walls, their surfaces stacked with books and knickknacks. Not the kind of things that a decorator would put out, but rather the sort that would be collected and displayed by someone who traveled a lot and collected memorabilia. Replicas of Greek Cycladic art sat side by side with bobble heads of famous musicians and composers.

There was little doubt. He may not stay in the house anymore, but he most definitely lived here.

As Ward shut the door behind her, she turned her attention back to him just in time to see him sliding his phone into his pocket. He was dressed in well-worn jeans and a gray V-neck sweater. The kind a woman automatically wanted to stroke and cuddle against.

He smiled faintly and, for the first time since she'd met him, looked a little self-conscious. "If he asks," Ward said, "can you tell Chase I moved back into the house?"

His request was so unexpected, Ana could do little more than shrug. "I…sure, I guess. Is he going to ask?"

"He might. He gave me hell a year ago when he found out I'd moved out."

What was she supposed to say to that? She'd never lost a spouse. So she could only imagine how he felt. How torn he must be, unable to move back into the house he'd shared with his wife, unwilling to sell it. Still, it wasn't her business or her place.

"You should call me then." He quirked an eyebrow in question, so she explained. "I'm a horrible liar. If you call me now, then I can at least tell him that and pretend I was never here."

Ward nearly laughed at Ana's statement. Her words were so blandly practical, he couldn't help but be amused. And yet, the sentiment seemed perfectly in-line with everything he knew about her. Once again, her stunning combination of exotic lush beauty and straitlaced practical clothing was a dichotomy he found all too appealing.

She wore a black-and-white houndstooth jacket cinched tight around her waist. She had an oversize leather tote slung over her shoulder. Once the door was closed behind her, she loosened the belt of her jacket to reveal slim black pants and a white business shirt that looked slightly rumpled after a day's wear. He found himself wanting to unbutton it to see what she had on beneath it.

He wanted to close the distance between them and tug loose her hair so that it tumbled around her shoulders. He wanted to run his hands through it and bury his nose in it. He ached to find out if her skin still held that intriguing combination of vanilla and cinnamon. If she still smelled like snickerdoodles.

And more than any of that, he wanted to kiss her. To feel her lips, hot and wet beneath his. To kiss her until her irritation turned to surprise and then keep on kissing her until that turned to desire. Until she wanted him with the same deep pounding need that he wanted her.

But of course, the one thing he didn't want to do was alienate her. Which kissing her would certainly do. Forget stripping her naked and lavishing her body with kisses.

Now, she was looking at him suspiciously. Little wonder since he was taking so long to respond. Instead of replying right away, he crossed into the kitchenette and pulled another tumbler from the cabinet.

He held it up in a gesture. "Do you drink tequila?"

She gave him a you're-an-idiot look, followed by a brief nod. "I mean, I don't do shots on a regular basis or anything. But

I've lived most of my life in Southern California. Pretty much everyone drinks tequila on occasion."

"Good point." He poured himself a finger and then one for her. He nudged hers across the counter.

She took a ladylike sip, a testament to her previous experience with Gran Patron. It was a sipping tequila.

He nodded in approval, then raised the glass in a silent toast and took a drink of his own, relishing the sharp burn down his throat. Then he set the tumbler down.

There was a part of him that wanted to tell her outright how much he wanted her. It was the same part of him that wanted to bend her over the table and plow into her right now. But he didn't think either technique would fully satisfy him. Instead, he started talking. Doing what he did best. Seducing her with the sound of his voice and his ability to weave a story.

"When you're a musician," he began. "Everybody wants to buy you drinks. Club owners, fans, other musicians. Right or wrong, I've been drinking tequila since I was fifteen. A lot of it is pretty nasty stuff. It's why you do shots, with salt and lime." He picked up his tumbler again and held it up so the light from the pendant over the bar shone through the glass. The liquid was as clear as water. Only the astringent sting of it in his nose indicated its seductive power. "But Gran Patron, it's the best sipping tequila in the world. You don't drink it in shots. You linger over it. You savor it."

In turn, she lifted her glass, took another sip and let it slide down her throat. He watched the delicate muscles in her neck shift beneath her skin as she swallowed. There was something innately erotic about watching her drink. Something about just being with her that soothed him.

Yes, she got in his face about Hannah's Hope, but he never felt like she was desperate for a chunk of him, the way he sometimes felt with people. That only added to her appeal. Only reinforced the gut-wrenching desire he felt for her.

Since she didn't say anything, he kept talking. "I've found women are a lot like tequila. When you're a musician, there's a lot of them around. Like cheap tequila, sometimes you indulge without lingering over them. Something you do just because it's there and it's available." He rolled the tumbler between his palms. "I loved my wife and I never once cheated on her, I was never even tempted. Why would I drink a shot of cheap tequila just because someone handed it to me when I had something worth savoring back at home."

He looked at her then, his expression darkening. He took another drink of the Patron and then asked as if it was only just now occurring to him, "Does that analogy offend you?"

She thought about it for a second, tilting her head to the side as she considered. While she could see how it might offend some people, it didn't bother her. "My father used to say that women are like Eskimos. You've heard the myth about Eskimos having forty words for snow? He said women were like that. We have hundreds of words for emotions. But men don't. They describe women like possessions because they have no other way to convey how desperately they need them."

Funny, she hadn't thought about that in a long time. Growing up, her parents lectured her endlessly about staying out of trouble. They were so afraid of her messing up her life and her future by doing drugs or having sex and getting pregnant. Her mother's lectures had been frequent, redundant and sometimes infuriating. But her father's words had stuck with her.

Don't sleep with a boy just because he says he loves you, he'd told her. *That's just a word boys will use to get you into bed. Wait for the boy who wants you enough that he's willing to wait. Wait for the boy who can't tell you how much he loves you. The boy who makes you believe it.*

And she'd never met a guy like that. And so here she was, a virgin at twenty-seven. Honestly, she'd begun to doubt love like that really existed. Yes, her parents were daily proof that it did, but she knew their relationship was rare. Maybe even a throwback to a simpler time and place. Maybe her generation had lost the ability to love so completely. Maybe decades of rising divorce rates and instant gratification had bred it out of them.

But listening to Ward compare Cara to sipping tequila, for the first time she believed love like that was really possible.

This man standing before her had faced every temptation imaginable. He had to have had countless opportunities to be unfaithful, but he'd loved his wife too much. Even now, three years later, he loved her too much to live in the house they'd shared together. He couldn't even discard her sunglasses.

How could that kind of devotion offend her, no matter what terms he couched it in?

She may not be able to understand the full depths of his grief. But she could respect it. And she certainly wasn't going to judge him for it. She hardly knew him well enough to have an opinion on what was a healthy way for him to grieve for his wife.

Circling back to his earlier request, she said, "If you don't want Chase to know you're living in the carriage house, he's certainly not going to hear it from me."

He nodded slowly and smiled. "Thanks."

But the smile looked sad. And a little rueful. Like he knew it was time to move on, but still wasn't sure if he wanted to.

She buried a wistful sigh. Her reasons for coming now seemed so self-serving in the face of his obvious grief. "I'm sorry I invaded your privacy. I should have left you alone." She set down the tumbler of tequila and headed for the door. He stopped her after only a step.

"Why did you come here?"

It sounded silly now. She had the unmistakable impression that the things he'd told her just now weren't the sort of thing he shared with just everyone. So she'd probably been wrong. And if she hadn't, so what? Why invade his privacy just to feed her insecurity? She'd worked with plenty of people she didn't like in the past. She was professional enough to do it this time around.

Except, of course, that she *did* like Ward. Immensely. And that, of course, was part of the problem. She didn't want there to be a likable person beneath the glamour of the megastar. But since there was, she'd have to figure out how to deal with him on her own.

Since Ward was still waiting for an answer, she smiled ruefully and said, "I thought you didn't like me."

However, when she looked up at Ward, she realized he'd gone completely still. He looked at her over the rim of his half raised tumbler with one eyebrow quirked. "What was that?" he asked, his voice pitched low.

That sultry tone sent a shiver down her spine, one she did her best to hide the effects of. She forced a nonchalant laugh. "It sounds silly now. But I thought maybe you'd been avoiding me."

"Avoiding you?" he asked. There was note of humor in his words. Like she'd just unwittingly repeated some private joke.

"Yes," she tried to keep her frustration out of her voice, but didn't succeed. "Avoiding me. You took a different flight out to Charleston, even though there wasn't really a board meeting. You haven't been at CMF, even though Stacy assures me that you're usually there every day that you're in town." His smile broadened, and her hands automatically went to her hips. "The other day at Hannah's Hope, you totally got in my face about whether I had a problem working with you. So, what? I'm not allowed to do the same thing?"

Her irritation crept back into her voice. Dang it, what was it about him that got under her skin?

She blew out a sigh and gave her shoulders a little roll to relieve the kinks of tension before adding, "It's not a big deal. I just thought I'd ask."

He slowly lowered his tumbler and grinned. "Let me get this straight. You think I'm avoiding you? Because I don't like you?"

She gritted her teeth for a second before answering. "Yes. And I don't want it to affect my work at—"

But before she could finish her sentence, he rounded the island and crossed the room to where she stood. She nearly gasped in surprise as he pulled her into his arms and kissed her.

Six

Kissing Ana was as close to heaven as a man like him could get. She smelled like snickerdoodles and tasted like his favorite tequila. Unless her skin was actually sprinkled with sugar, he just didn't see how she could get any better.

Her mouth was hot and moist and after an instant of surprise, unbelievably pliant and responsive. The purse she'd been holding slid off her shoulder and hit the floor and then her hands crept up around his neck to weave through his hair. She deepened the kiss, opening her mouth beneath his and boldly stroking her tongue against his teeth. His hand automatically sought her bottom, lifting to press her against his growing erection.

She tilted her hips forward, rubbing herself against him in a way that sent fissures of pure pleasure shooting through his body.

He hadn't meant for the kiss to get out of hand. Hell, he hadn't meant to kiss her at all. If she'd shown even the slightest resistance, he would have instantly let her go. But she melted against him, and so he clutched her to him even tighter and felt her shudder in response. He shoved her jacket off her shoulders and down her arms. Turning them around, he backed her up a step and then another, until her back was pressed to the wall beside the door. Her hips were anchored against his, but he wedged his hands between their bodies to flick open the buttons of her shirt, one by one. The shirt fell open to reveal a flesh-colored lacy bra.

He slipped his hand inside her shirt to the silky skin beneath. When he cupped her breast in his hand, she broke her mouth free, gasping in obvious pleasure. She threw back her head. With her mouth parted and damp, her eyes half-closed, and her breath coming in rapid bursts, she was the very picture of eroticism. Sex personified. Arousal in pure human form.

Her tongue darted out to lick her top lip and his erection leapt in response, straining against the zipper of his jeans.

If she was this turned on by such a little harmless groping, he couldn't imagine how she'd respond to all the things he wanted to do to her. He could almost imagine that the passion between them surprised her.

Then again, maybe it had. Just a few moments ago, she'd thought he didn't like her. She'd thought he was avoiding her.

Instantly, two parts of him were at war. One part that wanted to strip her pants from her body, pull her panties down around her knees and plunge his fingers deep inside of her. He wanted to find her clitoris and stroke it until she was mindless with passion. He wanted to suck it into his mouth and drive her mad.

But the other part of him—the last few shreds of his logical mind—knew that this wasn't the time. For any of that.

Ana was no cheap shot of…no, he stopped himself mid-thought. It felt wrong, somehow, to think of Ana in the same way he'd thought of Cara. They were too distinct. The comparison served neither of them well.

Ana was her own woman. Completely different from Cara. If Cara had been fine tequila, crafted, elegant and expensive, then Ana was…maybe the perfect margarita. A little salty, a whole lot of sweet and plenty of tart to balance it out. None of it hiding the drink's powerful punch. All of the ingredients working in harmony to produce a whole that was nearly irresistible.

But still the fact that he would even think of both women in the same thought made him distinctly nervous. Cara had held his heart, his career, hell, his entire life in her hands. And look how long it had taken him to get over that. No way was he ready for that again.

Nevertheless, Ana deserved more than a quick coupling against the wall. She certainly deserved the truth.

He stepped away slowly, waiting until her feet were firmly back on the ground, before turning away and plowing a hand through his hair. Christ, how had he lost control so fast?

Squeezing his eyes shut, he finally admitted the truth. "I wasn't avoiding you because I didn't like you, I avoided you because of this."

He looked back over his shoulder and took in the sight of her. She still stood with her back against the wall. Her breasts were rising and falling with each labored breath she pulled into her lungs.

With her shirt hanging open to reveal her perfect breasts encased in skimpy lace, she looked like his wildest fantasies come to life.

Her gaze still looked dazed and unfocused, proof that she didn't yet comprehend what he was saying.

"I was afraid of this," he admitted. "I knew the chemistry between us was palpable. I didn't want to come on too strong. To ruin our working relationship."

"Oh." She seemed to realize suddenly that her shirt was still unbuttoned. Her fingers went to work fumbling on the problem, but her breath still came in rough drags and her normally quick mind seemed to be working at half speed, which was still faster than his tequila-addled one.

He was lucky he'd been able to stop at all.

He crossed back to the kitchen, emptied his tumbler into the sink and then got himself a fresh glass of ice water. Since she looked about as befuddled as he felt, he got her one, too.

She followed him into the galley kitchen and accepted the glass, shaking her head as if to clear it. "So you've been avoiding me because you like me?" Then she held up her hand to ward off some protest she imagined he was about to make. "Forget I said that. That presupposes that affection and lust are somehow tied together."

"Ana—" he started to protest.

"No. It's okay." She smiled in a wobbly I'm-a-brave-little-trouper sort of way. Then she raised the water glass and drank it in quick, successive gulps. Like she needed to be doused with something icy. "So you want me, but you don't want to want me. Do I have that right?"

"Let's just say, yes, I want you. But sex complicates things. And I don't want to hurt you."

She set the glass down on the granite counter with a thud. "You're assuming you could hurt me."

Her naïveté was charming. "Yes, I am assuming that." Maybe he should feign modesty, but in truth, he knew her emotions would have little to do with the man he really was. "I've been a celebrity a lot longer than you've been dealing with celebrities."

"That's not true," she argued vehemently. "I dealt with all kinds of celebrities when I worked in Hollywood."

"How many did you sleep with?"

Her cheeks turned a fiery red. "That's none of your business!"

So the answer was either a lot, or none. He'd bet none. "My point is, celebrities are very easy to fall in love with, but very difficult to love."

He wasn't a particularly likable guy. He didn't know if he ever had been, back before Cara got sick, but he certainly wasn't now. It was a common malady among the famous. People fell in love with their fantasy rather than the person who was standing right in front of them, making their life miserable.

When she looked ready to protest again, he pressed his finger to her mouth to quiet her. "I don't want to hurt you. I don't want you falling in love with me and then one day waking up and realizing that I'm not the man you really wanted me to be. That wouldn't be fair to you."

She frowned, her gaze a little too insightful. "It sounds to me like that wouldn't be fair to either of us."

"You're a sweet kid, Ana. I don't want to hurt you."

Her gaze narrowed at his use of the word *kid*. He'd known it would. She wasn't a woman who took well to diminutives. There was more than one way to drive a woman away.

She jerked away from his touch, her gaze blazing and went to swipe her jacket off the floor. "So where does that leave us?" she asked, her tone tinged with defiance.

He shrugged. "We still have to work together for Hannah's Hope. Right now, while we're starting up, the board's involvement is pretty heavy. I don't see any way around that. But once things are underway, it'll slow down. In a year or so, I can step aside and you can find a new board member."

But her expression slowly darkened as he spoke and by the time he finished, he knew she was going to make this harder than it needed to be.

She shoved her arms back into the sleeves of her jacket, and slowly stalked toward him. "I meant, where does that leave us. Personally. You're convinced I'm some kind of delicate flower who can't handle being involved with you. But you're wrong. I can handle anything I want to handle."

He couldn't help smiling at her bravado. And her choice of words. He should probably walk calmly away from that innuendo, but, damn it, he just couldn't. "Am I to assume you want to handle me?"

She arched an eyebrow, opened her mouth as if to speak, then seemed to think better of it. After giving him an assessing stare, she admitted, "I don't know."

That careful consideration made him nervous. A quick *yes,* he could have easily dismissed. That need to pull her into his arms and devour her still pounded through him, but the cadence of it had slowed a little. It was controllable now. Gazing deep into her inky eyes, he could read nothing in them except the lingering traces of her passion.

She pressed her fingertips to her temples and squeezed her eyes shut for a second. Like she was trying to block out the chatter of her internal debate.

A second later, she opened her eyes, her expression just as

confused. "I know I don't want to walk away from this. I don't want to walk away from you."

"Hey," he said trying to keep his tone playful. "It's not every day a celebrity saunters into your life, right?"

The hard edge in his voice surprised him. He'd long ago gotten over any annoyance over the nail-a-celebrity scorecard some women seemed to keep. And he didn't really think Ana was that kind of woman. But apparently, he still needed to hear that straight from her.

"It's not that." Annoyance flickered across her face. "Which you know."

And to be fair, he did know. It wasn't about that for her. Obviously. She'd worked in Hollywood. Met plenty of stars bigger than him in her life before Hannah's Hope. He didn't know how she'd managed to escape male attention in Hollywood. Thank God her figure was lush and curvaceous. Maybe in the land of skinny starlets the men there were all too stupid to appreciate Ana's figure. Though it was the spark of passion that really spoke to him. Her devotion to Hannah's Hope. He was less confident about what attracted her to him.

"Then what is it?" he pressed, surprised by his desperate need to hear her voice her attraction. He wasn't generally the kind of guy who needed to have his ego stroked.

She shrugged. "I'm not sure. But would it be so bad if we let it run its course? If we waited to find out?"

He let out a low grumble of displeasure. Again, he shook his head. "I'm not going to risk your heart out of curiosity."

"It's not your heart to decide."

He cupped her cheek in his palm. "Here's the thing. Celebrities are very easy to fall in love with. But we're almost impossible to love."

Sadness flickered across her face. For an instant, he thought it was because she thought he was blowing her off. But then her lips curved in an almost smile and he realized he'd mistaken sympathy for sorrow.

"Yes. You said that already." She bumped up her chin and met his gaze boldly. "But I'm not going to fall in love with you."

Despite his grim mood, he found himself smiling. "You're not?"

"No. Not even a little bit."

"You promise?"

Her smile turned a little mischievous. "Cross my heart and lock it with a padlock."

He still knew he should say no. He should push her out the door. Shut it behind her. Put her on a plane back to San Diego and never see her again.

This instinct he had to possess her, to keep her with him…it wasn't good for her. And he was a selfish bastard for giving in to it.

But what could he say. He wanted her, plain and simple. And it had been too long since he'd wanted anything. He'd grown greedy during his emotional abstinence and if she didn't have the good sense to leave, he didn't have the strength to make her.

"Okay," he agreed.

She smiled broadly, as if she'd won some kind of prize. Like she was the lucky one here, when in reality he was the one who would walk away the winner. He would inevitably disappoint her and she'd be lucky if she didn't get crushed.

She rose up on her toes, her hand sneaking around his neck, but he carefully dodged her grasp.

"But we take it slowly," he explained. "I may want to take you to bed and do all kinds of sinful things to your body. But we're not going to do that now."

"Oh." Her eyes widened. And then a blush streamed up her cheeks.

Either he'd shocked her with his bluntness—which was entirely possible—or she genuinely hadn't considered the possibility that if he started kissing her again, he might not be able to stop.

She went rapidly from confusion to surprise to embarrassed satisfaction. She didn't quite meet his gaze as she nodded. "Okay. So where do we go from here?"

"We go to dinner."

"Dinner?"

"Yeah." He grabbed her hand and tugged her toward the

door. He snagged a set of keys from the console. "Neither of us has eaten. Public is much better. I don't trust myself alone with you."

Ward let her drive to dinner. Though he'd only had two shots, it had been on an empty stomach since he hadn't yet dug into the take-out leftovers. And she'd only had a sip of her drink. His sensibility on the subject impressed her. A lot of men viewed asking someone else to drive as an affront to their masculinity. Not Ward.

He let her choose which car she drove, offering up one of his instead of her mild-mannered rental. Standing in the bay of the carriage house garage, she considered her options. A bright Tesla—a powerful, all-electric sports car. Another Lexus hybrid, identical to the one he drove in California. And a fully-restored Hudson Hornet, all patent leather and gleaming chrome. Its sleek lines both elegant and powerful, giving the impression that it was a wild beast, poised to pounce on some prey.

She'd probably never again have the opportunity to drive a machine like this. Only an idiot would choose her rented sedan under the circumstances.

In many ways, this thing with Ward was just like that. All her life, she'd put off getting involved romantically. She'd held herself aloof. Made the sensible decision. In short, she'd been driving a sedan her whole life.

And now, here she was faced with ultimate temptation.

No, she'd never have a real relationship with Ward. His heart belonged to another. Despite that, he desired her. His passion when they'd kissed had been unmistakable, even to a relative neophyte like her. Moreover, he'd stirred within her feelings that no one else ever had. If all she could have was his passion, then she'd make do with that.

She had no illusions he'd ever love her, but that was okay. As long as she kept her heart out of it, she could indulge her body's desires. How could she resist? Geez, she figured there was even a chance he was experienced enough that he'd barely notice taking her virginity when the time came. At the very least, she knew the passion between them would burn hot enough to make giving it up worth it.

As she slid behind the wheel of the Hornet, pure adrenaline shot through her. It was very likely that driving this classic muscle car would ruin her for other cars forever. She didn't care. This was a once in a lifetime chance and she was going to seize it with both hands.

Dinner was a laid-back affair at a local diner wedged between a martial arts studio and a pub. It was enough of a dive that no one would just wander in off the street. Only a pretty adamant recommendation would get a newcomer through the door. But inside, it was clean and well lit. The owner—a boisterous Greek man—immediately came over to welcome Ward and clap him soundly on the arm. The other customers glanced in their direction, but otherwise ignored them, a sure sign Ward was a regular.

She couldn't help but smile when Ward slid into the red Naugahyde booth and his bench scooted a few inches back. Apparently, the man just couldn't sit down without moving furniture. Her amusement shifted to nervousness when she slid in opposite him and his legs brushed against hers. With his arm stretched out along the back of the bench, he seemed to fill the space so completely she could barely focus on reading the menu, let alone on making a decision about what to eat.

She allowed Ward to order for her and they feasted on spicy lamb hamburgers dripping with tzatziki sauce and served with fries and breaded zucchini. Over dinner, they spoke mostly of their plans for Hannah's Hope and his work with CMF.

There was an intimacy to sharing food with Ward that unsettled her. She didn't date much, having learned early in life avoiding romantic entanglements meant avoiding the physical advances that inevitably followed. So she wasn't used to the experience of sitting across from someone in a cramped booth. Of having her fingers brush his when they both went for the same fry or having him reach across the table with his napkin to dab at the tzatziki sauce she dribbled on her chin.

It wasn't until they were back in the car that she had the courage to ask the question she'd been plagued by ever since arriving in Charleston.

"Tell me something." Her voice sounded strained, but she tightened her hands on the steering wheel and pressed on. "Cara died of breast cancer."

She glanced in his direction, in the flickering light of the passing streetlight, she saw that he'd gone completely still. His expression was carefully blank.

She waited for him to respond, maybe to confirm what she already knew, but he said nothing, so she continued, "All the charities that the Cara Miller Foundation works with…none of them are cancer related. None for survivors or education or research—"

"That's what she wanted," he said abruptly.

Clearly, she'd crossed some sort of line. "I'm sor—"

"Don't be. I—" Then he released a sigh of pent-up emotion. "I'm not used to talking about it." Then he gave a wry chuckle. The kind without any humor at all. He scrubbed a hand down his face. "I talk about her all the time. But I never talk about her cancer. She never wanted to honor the cancer. Didn't want to give it an important place in her life. She figured it stole the last few years of her life, she wanted her death to be hers alone. She wanted her legacy to be helping children."

Ana considered his words. In a way, it made sense. She'd known a makeup artist back in Hollywood, a cancer survivor who devoted all of her free time to volunteer work for the American Cancer Society. She did relays and fundraising. All her friends were people she'd met through support groups. They were an amazing and inspirational group of men and women. But cancer was like another member of their little group. A living, breathing entity that never left them. Honoring cancer. That was the perfect word for it.

So, yeah, Ana could understand why Cara hadn't wanted that. Still, looking at Ward, she sensed he wasn't wholly comfortable with his wife's decision.

"But—" she prodded.

He slanted a look at her. "But what?"

"I just…" His gaze narrowed and she shrugged. "Yeah, that was her decision, but how did you feel about that?"

The second the question was out of her mouth, she regretted it. It was an intensely personal question. One she had no business asking and even less business knowing the answer to.

He lifted his shoulders in a shrug, but the car was too dark for her to gauge his expression.

"It wasn't my decision," he said. After a minute, he added, "Besides, I like working with kids. They make it worth it."

As she pulled to a stop at a light, she glanced at him in surprise. A smiled teased at his lips. His hands rested on his knees, tapping out a silent tune. She'd had to move the bench seat of the car close to the dash in order to reach the Hornet's pedals and now there was barely room for his long legs, making her profoundly aware of how much bigger he was than she.

"Do you work with kids often?" she asked because it seemed a safer question than trying to press him for more answers about Cara. Crossing that line once was enough for one evening.

"Not often," he answered. "I travel enough that I don't want any kid depending solely on me. But sometimes it just makes sense. Like with Ricky."

He threw out the name like Ricky was someone she should know. "Ricky?" she prodded.

"He wandered into Hannah's Hope the other day, during a school day. He's—I don't know—thirteen, fourteen maybe." Ward paused to gesture toward the coming intersection. "Turn left here." Then he continued his story. "Oddly enough, he wanted information about how to get his mother signed up for the new GED prep class that Omar is going to be teaching. He's worried about his mother's job prospects."

"That's perceptive," she said, shifting the Hornet into lower gear to pull out of the turn. "On the other hand, a lot of boys with single mothers are very protective of their moms."

"I know I was," Ward admitted.

She was tempted to press him for more information, but knew she'd pushed too much into his personal life for one night. "So you decided to mentor him?" she asked. "You were in town less than a week. When have you had time to mentor a kid?"

He chuckled. "I haven't actually mentored him yet. I've only met him that one time. But I could tell he was going to be tricky. He was there on a Friday morning. I told him I could get his mother the help she needed, but he'd have to stay in school himself. To make sure he's holding up his end of the bargain, he's going to come to Hannah's Hope when she does. But Ricky told me bluntly that he wasn't going to waste time with some meddling do-gooder. So I told him I'd mentor him after school. I could tell if I didn't hook him right away, we'd never see him again. So I agreed to meet him on Thursday afternoon. We'll see how it goes."

His admission grabbed at something inside of her and squeezed. Friday had been the day of the brainstorming session. He must have gotten in earlier even than she'd thought. How many men would voluntarily spend their evenings mentoring a troubled teen? Not enough, that was for sure. How many rich celebrities would do it? Almost none. At least none that she'd met.

"That's very generous of you," she said, her voice surprisingly tight.

Ward gave a little noncommittal grumble, as if uncomfortable with her praise. "We'll see how it turns out. I think he only agreed because I happened to have Dave's guitar with me and Ricky wanted to play it."

Her head jerked around to search his face in the darkness. Which was about as futile as trying to understand him. "You had Dave's guitar? Why?"

He gave a chuckle. "Not because I've been secretly recording a new album and was planning on using Hannah's Hope to promote it. If that's what you're worried about."

She felt her cheeks burning, suddenly aware of how ridiculous her accusations from that first day sounded. And feeling very much like he could see her better in the darkness than she could see him.

"Ward, about that, I'm—"

"I was joking," he said gently.

"Oh. Okay."

He gave another gesture toward an upcoming block and she maneuvered the car onto his street.

"Why not the Alvarez?" she asked tentatively.

"What?"

"If you are playing guitar again, then why not the Alvarez?"

"I wouldn't say I'm really playing it." There was a diffidence to his voice. As if he himself wasn't sure how to answer the question.

"Do you ever miss it?" she asked as she steered the car into his driveway.

He didn't answer, but pulled the automatic door opener from the glove box.

She waited while the carriage house doors cranked open and to fill the noticeable silence, she started talking.

"I started sewing because of my *abuela*. She could make anything, usually just by looking at it. Emma's mother, Denise, had bought her these beautiful dresses. Spent a fortune on her clothes. Emma couldn't bear to get rid of them after her mom died, so *Abuela* reworked them so Emma could wear them for years. Eventually, Emma started to bring her pictures of things she'd seen in a magazine and *Abuela* would make her clothes, too."

Ana coaxed the car into its spot and cut the engine. Then she shifted in her seat, bringing her leg onto the bench beside her as she faced him. Opening the garage door had triggered an overhead light, which cast the hard planes of his face in interesting shadows, but did little to reveal more of his mood.

"She taught me to sew when I was ten. It was something we did together. Even now that she's gone, I feel closest to her when I'm sewing. I still like to make my own clothes. It's the one thing I miss about being a costume designer."

Ward quirked an eyebrow. "That's what you regret about leaving Hollywood? Sewing is the only thing you miss?"

She chuckled. "Well, that and the fact that I never got to wear any of those gorgeous clothes I made." She held out the keys to the Hornet and dropped them into his hand. "That's why I was asking about the Alvarez. It was such an important part of your life for so long. I can't believe you don't miss it."

He carefully reached up and set the keys on the dashboard and then grabbed her hand from where it rested on her leg. "I'm not really interested in talking about the Alvarez."

She stilled instantly, her breath caught in her chest. His hand was warm, his fingertips rough as he ran them along her palm. Pressing her lips tightly together, she swallowed and forced her gaze from their joined hands to his face. "What do you want to talk about?"

A smiled played at his lips. "Maybe I don't want to talk."

He gave her hand a gentle tug. Heart pounding, she scooted across the bench toward him. Waiting for him to lower his mouth to hers, she felt as though she could barely breathe. And she was pretty sure that oxygen was overrated anyway. She didn't need it. Not the way she needed him.

Seven

He'd meant to give Ana a quick kiss and then send her on her away. But the second her lips touched his, it was as though a fire had sparked between them. She met his kiss with the same vibrant passion she'd brought to each of their arguments. She was all heat and emotion. She tasted of the sweet tea she'd drunk at dinner and the salt caramel gelato she had for dessert.

Her passion was so intense, so ardent as to be almost clumsy. Her tongue met his boldly, stroke for stroke. Her hands cupping the back of his head as she angled her mouth over his. Her awkward fumbling aroused him far more than a skilled seduction would have. His blood pounded through his veins, stirring his erection. She shifted her body this way and that, as if desperate to rub against him but unsure how to negotiate around the confines of the front seat.

He reached a hand down to the lever beneath the bench seat, gave it a tug and pushed the seat back as far as it would go. Then he stretched his legs out in front of him. Hooking his hand behind her knee, he pulled her onto his lap so she straddled him.

She groaned in approval, rubbing the juncture of her legs

against his growing erection. She tore her mouth from his, throwing her head back and gasping aloud. Grinding her hips against his, she gave a visible shudder.

Combined with the delightful pressure against his penis, the sight of her arousal was so erotic, he nearly came right there.

Still struggling to rein in his growing passion, he watched helplessly as she shrugged out of her jacket. He nearly cheered when her fingers reached for the buttons of her shirt. But some tiny shred of sanity made him grab her hand to stop her.

As gently as he could, he pushed her off his lap, sprung the door open and climbed from the car.

"Ward, wait—" she gasped.

He leaned down to talk to her through the open door to the car. She'd scooted to her side, her back pressed against the driver's side door. Clutching her jacket to her chest, she looked confused, delightfully rumpled, her arousal evident in her bruised, moist lips and wide eyes. He sucked in a deep breath, trying to regain control over his reaction, but unfortunately, the interior of the car was laden with her sweet scent.

"Get out of the car," he said gently.

She hurried from the car, but he held out a hand to stop her from closing the distance between them.

"I don't understand," she asked, the confusion on her face taking on a hurt look.

He was tempted to reach for her again. To offer comfort. But if he reached for her again, he knew how it would end, with the two of them naked, upstairs in his bedroom. Or, hell, maybe they wouldn't even make it that far. Maybe he'd take her up against the wall by his front door. Or just press her down over the hood of the Hornet, shove down her pants and plunge into her from behind.

As gut-wrenchingly tempting as any or all of those fantasies were, he didn't want their first time together to be like that.

He wanted to savor her. To lavish her with attention. To spend hours learning her every nook and cranny. But he wasn't going to do that tonight.

"I just—" he began, then broke off and sucked in another breath. "Let's take it slow, okay? Like we agreed."

"Okay." She nodded. But then took another step toward him.

He held up a hand to ward her off. "Whoa."

"I'm okay with slow," she said.

"I meant, let's take the relationship slow. Not, let's slowly hop into bed."

"Oh." Comprehension spread across her expressive face. She frowned. "Oh," she repeated, sounding miserable.

"There's no rush. Tomorrow night, we'll go back to Vista del Mar. We'll see what happens there."

Her frown only deepened. "I guess that's okay."

It would have to be. Despite her eagerness, he sensed that she wasn't as experienced as she wanted him to believe. Which only made her more vulnerable to him. He didn't want to rush into a sexual relationship that she wasn't ready for. Moreover, he didn't want her to rush into it and then regret it later. And she almost certainly would regret it.

Women who got involved with stars nearly always did.

Sure there were some women who could handle a one-night stand with a man they barely knew. He'd certainly been involved with plenty of those women. But Ana wasn't that type. The fact that they would have to work together only complicated matters further.

Which was precisely why he wanted to take things nice and slow. There was a good chance she was going to see past his finely crafted layer of bull to the man beneath. When she did, he'd let her go. Maybe that would happen sooner rather than later, but whenever it did happen, he wanted her to have as few regrets as possible.

He couldn't stand it if one more woman regretted being with him.

By the time she returned to Vista del Mar the following evening, Ana still wasn't positive she'd made the right choice when she'd decided to date Ward. But after spending a day and a half constantly in his company—after seeing firsthand all he'd accomplished with CMF, after having him escort her around Charleston, where he was universally treated with affectionate respect—after all of that, she'd definitely reached one conclusion. She may not have made the right choice. But she'd really made the only choice.

How could she turn him down?

It would have been impossible.

But she could certainly appreciate how tenuous their situation was. And for that reason, she told him on the flight home that she didn't want anyone at Hannah's Hope or in Vista del Mar knowing about their burgeoning—but still very undefined—relationship. Her trust that he would follow her wishes was absolute. That same stalwart honor that had made him warn her off meant he would respect her request.

Still, even though she was not yet ready to share their relationship with others, she couldn't hide the improvement it made to her mood. She tried not to be too bubbly when she showed up at Hannah's Hope the day after her return.

"So how was the trip with Mr. Fabulous?" Christi asked, hovering in the open doorway.

Ana ducked her head, trying to hide from her friend's too astute gaze. "It was great. Charleston was completely charming."

"Really?" Christi asked. "I thought you were dreading it."

"Oh… Well, sure." Of course she had been dreading it. Back when she thought that Ward was a class-A jerk. Back when she'd wanted to believe the worst of him. So now she was stuck wondering how to change her tune without revealing what had really happened in Charleston. Her gaze pinned to her keyboard, she said, "Great restaurants, lots of Southern charm, nice people, beautiful old buildings. What's not to love?"

Christi's eyebrows shot up. "I'm surprised. Last I heard you thought it was going to be… What was the phrase you used? A ridiculous waste of time. So was it?"

Ah. Finally, a truly safe topic. She launched into a detailed explanation of how the CMF office worked. That was stuff she could talk about until the cows came home. She just carefully avoided saying anything about Ward. If she so much as mentioned his name then she might blush crazy red and embarrass herself.

After a few minutes of listening to Ana enthuse about CMF, Christi's eyes started to glaze over. She edged toward the office door. "Hey," she finally interrupted. "I think I'm going to run out for coffee. You want anything?"

"Nope." Ana smiled, satisfied that she'd sufficiently thrown Christi off track.

At the door, Christi paused for a second. "You seem to be getting along better with Mr. Fabulous."

Ana feigned a casual shrug. "He's not so bad."

Christi winked. "Glad to hear it. I thought for sure you'd go ballistic when you heard about that red carpet thing."

And with that, Christi was gone and Ana was left staring at the open doorway with her mouth open. To the empty room she asked aloud, "What red carpet thing?"

The room did not answer.

She considered calling Christi back, but for what? She could only badger her employee so much and right now she feared coming off like a lunatic. If Christi had expected her to go ballistic over it, then it couldn't be good.

She fished her cell phone out of her purse and called Ward, then left a message when he didn't answer. After a few minutes of tapping her fingers on the desk and fuming silently, she dug out Jess's number and called him, too.

"Great!" he said as soon as he answered. "I was trying to get ahold of you."

He couldn't have been trying very hard, since neither her cell phone nor her office phone had rung in the past thirty minutes. It didn't seem wise to point that out. "Oookay," she said blankly.

"Do you want the limo to pick you up at Hannah's Hope or at your house?"

"The limo?" she asked.

"Sure, the limo." Jess kept talking, oblivious to the warning tone in her voice. "Ward thought maybe it should pick you up at

Hannah's Hope. Protect your privacy. And he was worried you wouldn't have an appropriate dress."

"A dress appropriate for what?" she spoke slowly, trying to rein in her temper. As if it wasn't bad enough that Ward hadn't called her himself to ask her out to this supposed red carpet thing, she had to hear about it from his assistant.

"The second annual Hudson Pictures Breast Cancer Research Fundraiser. Ward is going to have a dress sent over."

"I…" She fumed, stumbling over her words in surprise. The Hudsons owned one of the most prestigious studios in Hollywood. They represented the glamorous world of old Hollywood. For decades, they'd hosted a Valentine's Day ball. Lillian Hudson, the matriarch of the family, died a few years ago after battling breast cancer. Since then, the Hudsons had retooled the Valentine's Day party as a fundraiser for breast cancer research. The invitations were highly coveted and almost impossible to come by. "Why would I need a dress for the Hudsons' Party?"

Finally, Jess picked up on her shock and confusion. "Ward hasn't talked to you yet, has he?"

"No."

"Ah, crap." Jess started talking rapidly. "I've bungled this. He intended to talk to you first. When you called me, I just assumed—"

"Stop," she cut Jess off midbumbling explanation. "Why don't you just tell me where I can reach him and I'll talk about it with him."

"I can't do that," Jess said meekly.

"You can tell me I'm being sent an appropriate dress for some event I'm supposed to go to with him, but you can't tell me where he is?"

"Oh, I can tell you where he is," Jess hastened to correct her, as if to prove his worth as an assistant. "You're just not going to be able to talk to him."

She blew out a long, frustrated sigh. "And why is that?" she asked slowly.

"Because he's at the recording studio." Jess's tone sounded

sheepish. "Look, Ana, I know it's awkward when you can't get ahold of him."

"Awkward. That about covers it."

"But trust me," Jess continued. "Ward is planning a very romantic evening."

And that's when Ana went ballistic. Quietly and internally, but still she went ballistic. Because not only was their secret relationship no longer secret, but it had gone from a passionate fling to something that included romantic evenings, limo rides and red carpets. Which felt like something much more complicated that mere sex.

By nine o'clock that evening, Ana was about halfway through her glass of wine and flipping through the channel guide on her television when she saw a VH1 program that would ruin her attempts to put Ward firmly out of her mind. If she tuned in she'd have the very surreal experience of watching on her flat screen a man she'd been kissing less than twenty-four hours ago.

She stared for a long minute at the name of the show on her screen. Instead, she found a movie playing, and settled down to watch that. Two minutes in, with a hefty gulp of wine, she changed the channel to VH1. Forty minutes later, she'd given up all semblance of being a casual watcher. Feeling voyeuristic and just a tad obsessive, she'd scooted to the edge of her seat and sat with her elbows propped on her knees. They'd already covered Ward's rapid rise to stratospheric fame and were now analyzing his distinctive musical style, how his detailed fret work on an electrified acoustic guitar combined with his gravelly voice to create a sound unlike any other musician.

But honestly, she knew all that already. She'd been enough of a fan before he'd come to Hannah's Hope that she knew much of his professional history. What held her riveted tonight was the footage of him on stage.

Of course, she'd seen him on stage before. Back when she'd been going to school in New York, she'd seen him perform more than once. But of course, things were different now. And the focused, tight angle shot of him sitting on an otherwise empty stage gave her a perspective she'd never before seen.

Usually his band included a drummer, a percussionist and a bassist. However, he had a few signature songs that he played alone. Just a guy on a darkened stage making one guitar sound as complex and layered as a whole band. Watching that footage now, she was blown away—all over again—by his sheer talent. By the tremendous amount of work that it must take to master any instrument with such skill. And by the intense concentration and sheer joy on his face as he played.

He was a genius. A virtuoso. And he'd given it all up.

Why?

Why would a man who—

Her doorbell rang, shattering her concentration. She guiltily leapt from her spot on the sofa like she'd been caught peeping. Her remote went flying. She caught it midair and punched Pause on her way to the door.

She flipped on her porch light and threw open the dead bolt. Her neighbor, Marla, a student at the local college had a habit of locking herself out of her house. But the person at the door was not Marla.

In fact, Ana had to stare at him for a solid minute before recognition set in. "Ward?" She gaped stupidly.

He looked completely different than he had any other time she'd seen him. Gone was the casually elegant rock star. He now wore a scruffy cowboy hat pulled low over his eyes. His cowboy boots had seen better days and his stained and ripped jeans were one step away from the trash heap. But more than just his clothes had changed. There was an air of beaten-down resignation about him. Like he was down on his luck and one kick in the teeth away from desperation.

His transformation was just shy of miraculous. The first day they'd met, in his pricey cargo pants and five-hundred-dollar sunglasses, he looked like a star foolishly trying to blend in. Now, he looked like a different person.

"I…" she fumbled, still confused.

He said nothing, but his head gave a tiny nod toward her neighbor's house and his eyes shifted in that direction.

She followed his gaze, only to realize Marla was walking up the path to her house—keys in hand, thank goodness—and was shooting curious glances their way.

Ward leaned forward slightly. "Repeat after me, loudly."

"What?"

"This is very unusual," he whispered. "I never see clients at my house."

Like an idiot, she stared blankly at him. Then glanced at Marla again, who had stopped and was staring at them both with her head tilted to the side. Even though it was dark, Marla had left the porch light on, allowing Ana a clear view of the other woman's expression of curiosity.

Abruptly, she repeated his words, her voice sounding stiff.

He gave a brief nod, then fed her another line.

"But under the circumstances," she added more loudly, "you can come in. I'll see what I can do to help."

His lips curved into a smile, giving her the impression her clumsy acting amused him. Figured.

"Gracias, señorita," he said. His Spanish had the flowing accent of a native speaker.

She swallowed her annoyance and stepped back to let him into her house. The moment when she could have refused to even let him in had passed in a blur of playacting and deception.

The second the door closed behind him, his shoulders straightened and the air of despair dissipated. He knocked his hat back an inch with his thumb and grinned like this was the most fun he'd had in months.

"What are you doing here?" she demanded, annoyance struggling back to the surface like indigestion.

"You're the one who said we should keep our relationship private."

"You want to bring me to a red carpet event where there will be oodles of photographers, but you dress in this elaborate getup just to stop by my house?"

He shrugged as if admitting the absurdity. Still, he snagged her wrist and reeled her in close, then trapped her there with his hands on her hips. "At the Hudsons' party, no one will think twice about us being together in a professional capacity. But I don't have any excuse to be at your house after nine on a weekday."

He plastered his lips to hers, gently invading her mouth with slow, even strokes of his tongue. His hand slipped up to rest on the bare skin of her back, his fingers teasing the sensitive flesh he found there. Her resistance melted under his gentle persuasion.

She felt a groan of pleasure rising in her throat. He took one step, edging her back toward the sofa. And then abruptly lifted his head.

"What's that?"

Startled by his sudden absence, she blinked away her confusion. Then followed his gaze to where it rested on a giant close-up of his face. Her own face instantly flashed hot. Ah, crap.

"That's, um…"

He pulled back and studied her face. "That's me."

Eight

Ward's tone sounded more amused than anything else.

Walking closer to the TV until the remote was within range and she could turn it off and bleep away the giant image of his face, she nodded with mock seriousness. "Yes. That's you." To cover her embarrassment, she added, "Come on in. I might as well offer you something to drink."

He pretended not to notice her reluctance, but crossed to her sofa, lowered himself to the seat, and stretched his legs out in front of him. He crossed his legs at the ankles and said, "Whatever you're having would be perfect."

"It's not fancy," she blurted. And then immediately regretted it, because she didn't know if she was talking about the ten-dollar wine or her used sofa. Or the fact that between the move and getting things set up at Hannah's Hope, her future dining room was full of unpacked boxes and her bookshelves were still empty.

"Not fancy sounds just about perfect."

By the time she returned with another glass of wine, she'd sufficiently pep-talked herself into believing that she did not care what he thought of her house. And she did not care if her living room was smaller (and more cheaply furnished) than the powder room in his mansion. After all, a man who lived in a garage apartment hardly had room to complain. And she did not care that she'd changed out of the professional jacket she'd worn earlier and now wore a workout tank and ten-dollar, wide-legged yoga pants that made her Latin hips look big.

She wasn't going to let herself be intimidated by his star status. The simple truth was, far more stood between them than her pedestrian taste in wine. She wasn't and would never be Cara Miller. In the end, that was what would drive them apart. Not her curvy hips.

But she couldn't help wishing that her heart hadn't started thundering at the sight of him sprawled out on her sofa when she stepped back through the doorway.

He'd rested his head against the back of the sofa. His eyes were closed, his hands resting on his perfectly flat abs. Her gaze took in his appearance again, since he wasn't looking. It was a good disguise, even if she didn't appreciate his efforts. Even the hair hanging down from under his cowboy hat looked darker.

Then he spoke without so much as cracking an eye. "It's flawless, isn't it?" His eyes opened and she saw humor in his gaze. "It's true what they say, the clothes make the man."

Embarrassment washed over her. Why had she just stood there staring at him like an idiot? Or, rather, like a giggly fan. But before she could think of something to say to hide her embarrassment, her phone rang.

"Please tell me you're not being held prisoner," Marla demanded the second Ana answered.

Ana laughed. "Hi, Marla. No, I'm not being held hostage." Ward quirked an eyebrow and she mouthed the words *my neighbor* to him.

"Are you sure?" Marla's voice sounded high-pitched and edgy.

Ana set her wine down on the coffee table. When she glanced up, it was to find Ward watching her carefully.

Quickly, she turned away and crossed to the window facing

Marla's house. She pulled back the gauzy curtain. Across the gap between their houses, which was a mere fifteen feet, she could see Marla standing at her own window, framed by the light of her own lamp. She stood there, cell phone pressed to her ear with one hand. Home phone handset in the other. She jiggled it like she was tempting a cat with a toy.

"I can call the cops on the landline if you need me to. We need a safe word! If he's there in the room with you and you can't talk, say watermelon. No, wait! That's too obvious. Say…'I'll see you in Sunday school.'"

"Marla, you're a kook. But a very good friend. And you read too many mystery novels. I'm not being held hostage."

"Are you sure? That guy looked a little dodgy."

"He's just a client," Ana said in her most reassuring voice.

"But you never see clients at the house," Marla protested.

"True. I haven't seen clients here. But…"

Just as she was fumbling for a reason, Ward leaned forward and waved to get her attention.

"My son is the hospital," he whispered.

"But his son is in the hospital," she repeated. Then she added, "He doesn't speak much English. The staff has him scared, even though he has nothing to be afraid of. It's complicated."

"You're sure?"

"Yes, I'm sure." She glanced in Ward's direction only to once again find him watching her. To hide her discomfort, she rolled her eyes. "Thank you for checking up on me. And I'll even call you tomorrow if it'll make you feel better."

"First thing in the morning. Promise?"

"I'll call you at seven."

"Hmm," Marla paused. "Nine would be better. I mean unless you need something. No, seven's fine. I mean, whenever."

"Thank you, Marla," Ana said before disconnecting.

"Your friend seems very…safety conscious." Ward chuckled.

"She's a good neighbor." She propped her hands on her hips, feeling suddenly protective of Marla, who, despite being a kook, was the best kind of neighbor and the first new friend she'd made since moving back to Vista Del Mar. "There's nothing wrong with that."

Ward held up his hands in a gesture of innocence. "I didn't say there was. It's nice. Refreshing, actually, to know there are still places where people watch out for each other."

Which was exactly how she felt about Vista del Mar. But even as she was considering launching into yet another lecture about the importance of Hannah's Hope, he nodded toward the TV. "So, you learn anything new?"

"Not much. They weren't very thorough. They didn't even mention Orange Kitty."

His eyebrows shot up. "How'd you know about Orange Kitty?"

"I lived in New York during college. I made it to a few Orange Kitty shows."

That had been the height of his career. Before Cara got sick. He'd toured most of the year, and split the rest of the time between their home in Charleston and their apartment in Manhattan. Whenever all the band members were in New York at the same time, they'd play in local venues, to small audiences under the name Orange Kitty.

He shook his head ruefully, a surprised smile on his face. "You must have been a hard-core fan to actually get out to an Orange Kitty show."

The Orange Kitty shows had never been publicized, being spur of the moment. And that wasn't the point, anyway. People either showed up by accident or heard about them by word of mouth.

"I once spent an entire night hitting bars all over Lower Manhattan because my friend had heard Orange Kitty was playing."

There was a hint of nostalgia in his smile. "And were we?"

"Not that time." Suddenly, her embarrassment spread and she felt as though she'd revealed far more than she'd meant to. She busied herself putting her remote away and fluffing a pillow. "I bet half the people in New York have stories like that."

He grabbed her hand and tugged her closer. She found herself

ooking at the topmost button of his ragged shirt, with far more
ntensity than such a bland pearlescent button deserved.

Slowly he tipped her head up, forcing her to meet his gaze.
"Until now, you've acted like you weren't a fan at all. Why?"

She wanted to pull herself out of his arms, but instead forced
herself to look him fully in the eyes. "That's obvious, right?"

"Not to me."

She shrugged. "I didn't want you to think I was just some
desperate fan-girl. That's…" she searched for the right word
"…creepy."

"It's never creepy knowing someone has enjoyed my
music."

There was a quiet sincerity to his voice. And she found
herself pouring out the question she'd been holding back since
Charleston. "So why don't you write music anymore? Why don't
you play?"

He dropped his hand and leaned back, his expression suddenly
distant.

"How do you know I don't?"

His tone was as cold as his gaze, but she pressed on. She was
too far past the line for it to matter now. "I saw the Alvarez.
At CMF. It's the only guitar you ever composed on. You may
have been carrying around your friend Dave's guitar, but I can't
imagine you composing on it."

He turned away from her and scrubbed a hand through his
hair. For a moment, she was certain that he was either going to
lie outright or tell her to mind her own damn business.

Instead, he leveled an assessing gaze at her and said, "Why
don't you tell me your theory."

She considered for a moment, gazing at the blank TV screen
where his face had been just moments ago. What was it he wanted
from her? She'd thought their relationship to be pure sex. She
hadn't expected him to show up on her doorstep in the evenings.
She hadn't expected romantic dates. She hadn't expected to be
telling him her theories about anything.

But since he'd asked for it, she found herself musing aloud.
The idea had come to her as she watched the show. And now

she couldn't bring herself to swallow her words, even though she knew it would be easier to keep her opinions to herself.

"Well, I think that's obvious. You don't play anymore for the same reason you don't live in the house in Harleston Village. You feel like your talent betrayed you. From the time you were a teenager, your talent got you everything you ever wanted. Fame, fortune, success. It was your path out of poverty. Not just for you, but for your mother, too." She nodded toward the screen. "It even helped win you Cara's love. But then, when you needed it most, it abandoned you. All the talent in the world couldn't save her life. Your wealth didn't matter. No amount of money could buy her a treatment, because nothing could cure her. Your gift betrayed you when you needed it most."

"That's ridiculous," he scoffed, but she could read the shock on his face, as if the idea were repugnant.

"Is it?" she prodded, trying to at least keep him talking so the idea would have a chance to sink in. "Stacy told me you haven't even picked up the Alvarez since Cara died. Before she got sick, it never left your side. You traveled with it everywhere you went. You wouldn't even leave it at the studio overnight. Now, you can barely even be in the same room with it."

"You're talking about it like it's a person. It's just a guitar. A piece of wood and some strings and a few electronics."

"You don't really believe that. It's more than just a guitar. It's the living embodiment of your talent. It's the heart and soul of your success as an artist. And you've turned your back on it just as clearly as it turned its back on you."

"I don't think that." His tone was quiet, but with so little emotion, she knew he had to be straining to keep it from his voice. "That's completely illogical."

"Of course it is. I'm talking about feelings, not logic. You're the one with the soul of a poet. You know better than anyone that there's no logic in the heart."

He met her gaze for a second, unnerved by the understanding he saw there. Damn, but she was perceptive. She'd pegged him so easily, it unnerved him.

Was she right? Was that why he hadn't touched the Alvarez since Cara died?

He didn't know. All he knew was that any desire he'd had to play the guitar had died with Cara. The bits of song that used to tease at the edges of his mind had disappeared. He'd even wondered if it was gone forever. Until he'd returned to California for this trip. But lately, while running on the beach or sitting in traffic, the music had started to come back to him. He didn't want to consider the possibility that it was tied to Ana.

Abruptly, he turned away, shoving aside all his thoughts about music. "Look, about the Hudsons' party, I'm sorry I didn't get a chance to call you and talk to you first."

"*That's* what you're sorry about?"

He purposely ignored the subtle emphasis she placed on *that's*. For now he'd had more than enough of her poking at his wounds. "Yes, I'm sorry. I got the call early this morning about the fundraiser. Jack Hudson heard I was in town and he gave me a call. I thought you'd be excited."

But her arms remained crossed firmly over her chest. "Why would I be excited about that? Ward, I hardly think—"

He could tell from her tone she was going to bring up the Alvarez. Instead of letting her, he deftly steered the conversation back to the party. "This is the first time I've gone in years, but it's always a great party. It should be fun."

Or maybe not so deftly, if the frown on her face was any indication.

After a second, she blew out a rough breath of air. "So that's how it's going to be?"

He knew exactly what she meant. Knew what she was asking for, and still he couldn't bring himself to respond. How could he explain to her what he didn't even understand himself?

She frowned, obviously distressed, but apparently willing to let him change the subject. "You forget, I worked in Hollywood for years. Those kinds of people don't impress me." Her voice sounded weary. Resigned to letting him manipulate the conversation.

"Have you met Jack and CeCe Hudson? They're nice people.

Yes, it's a red carpet, fundraiser thing. And I'm sure there'll be some people there who aren't wonderful. That's true in any crowd. But you should at least try to be open-minded about them."

She shot him a look of pure exasperation. "They could be Santa and Mrs. Claus and I still wouldn't want to go to their fundraiser. You've missed the point. I told you I wanted to keep our relationship a secret. And then you turn around and accept this invitation without even talking to me first. And to make matters worse, you have your assistant make arrangements before I've even agreed to go."

He found himself smiling despite her obvious ire. He kind of liked being chewed out by her. He crossed to stand in front of her and gently untangled her arms so he held both her hands in his.

"You're missing the bigger picture."

She gave a halfhearted tug to free her hands. The frown on her face softened slightly. "I think I see the picture pretty clearly."

Once again, he got the feeling that she was too damn perceptive. That she saw straight through his bull and knew precisely why he'd steered the conversation away from his musical career and toward the Hudsons' party.

"Do you? Because you must realize that this fundraiser is the perfect platform for talking about Hannah's Hope."

"It is?" She still looked skeptical.

"Yes, it is. I can chat up the charity to all the celebrities there. Plus, there will be reporters there. We can reach a larger audience than you'll ever be able to in Vista del Mar. Besides, the best part is, since I'll be there promoting Hannah's Hope, I have the perfect excuse to take you with me. The fact that we're together won't raise any eyebrows."

"I don't know about that."

"Well, I'm willing to risk it. Are you?" Instead of giving her a chance to answer, he tugged on her hands to pull her closer. "I don't mind keeping our relationship secret, but I want to be with you. You can't really blame me for wanting to spend time with my girlfriend, can you?"

She frowned, looking very much like she still wanted to argue with him.

So he pressed on. "I want to take you dancing and drink champagne with you. I want to spoil you. Why are you so afraid of letting me do that?"

Again she didn't answer right away and it frustrated him. He was used to dealing with people who were all too eager to let him shower them with life's luxuries. Yet here he was with Ana, who seemed to want nothing from him besides his company.

Maybe that should thrill him, but it didn't. She wasn't someone who would be fooled by smoke and mirrors. But after Cara's death, he wondered sometimes if there was anything left to him behind the illusions.

He didn't want Ana to find out. Hell, he didn't want to find out, either.

So he pulled out all the stops. There may not be anything behind the wizard anymore, but the wizard did still have a few moves of his own.

He trailed his hand up her arm. Tantalizing her skin with his touch. Slowly, he pulled her to him, and brushed his lips against hers. He felt the last tremors of her resistance melt away beneath his touch. She responded almost instantly to him, opening her mouth to his, arching to press her breasts against his chest. She was such a beguiling mixture of wide-eyed innocence and pure raw passion. And he ached with the pounding need to make her his.

But he forced himself to pull back. Drawing in deep breaths, he pressed his forehead to hers and reined in his self-control. They'd agreed to take things slow. That's what he wanted. In theory.

Stripping her naked in her living room and taking her on the sofa would not be taking it slow.

Finally, he asked, "So will you let me take you out or not?"

Her frown deepened to a scowl. "That sounds very romantic." She all but grumbled the word. Like romantic was about as appealing as finding slugs in her shoes. But after a long moment, she nodded. "Yes. I'll go with you to this Valentine's Day party."

But she still sounded doubtful. And by the time he left, he wasn't sure if she'd finally agreed because she really wanted to go with him or if the luster of dating a star was already starting to wear thin.

Ana knew she was in trouble the second the package arrived. No one had ever sent her a dress before. Still, she'd grown up watching old Doris Day movies and she'd seen enough of them to know that when a thirty-six by twenty-four inch box is couriered to your door, there's a fancy dress inside. Or maybe a mink coat. But no one wore real mink anymore.

In the movies, the delivery of the dress always preceded one of those whirlwind dates, where the hero whisks the heroine off to some exotic locale with the intent to seduce her. Inevitably, he failed. She returned home, virginity intact, but her beauty and charm—and stalwart defense of said virginity—inevitably won the hero's heart. That was the nice thing about being a movie heroine. You always came out on top. It was a good gig if you could get it.

But Ana had no illusions. She wasn't Doris Day. She wasn't even the Mexican-American Doris Day. And while she didn't cling to her virginity with any particular sentimentality, she did have her standards. And the deep-seated fear that if she did let Ward sweep her off her feet, she might never again find solid footing.

And so when the dress box arrived on Friday morning, she accepted it with a grim smile, but resisted opening it. After all, she had a perfectly acceptable black dress hanging in her closet.

By the time she and Emma had met at the Bistro after work, she'd almost forgotten about the box sitting ominously on her bed. Emma's wedding was in the morning and they were celebrating with nonalcoholic champagne. The ceremony would be quiet and small, with only family and a few close friends in attendance. Still, Ana couldn't be happier for her friend.

And so, Ana really had forgotten about the dress by the time

Emma came back by Ana's house to check out the new digs. Emma hadn't seen the house since Ana had moved in.

Naturally, when the impromptu tour reached the bedroom, the first thing Emma did was saunter over to the bed.

"What's this?" she asked. With her good hand, Emma struggled to get enough leverage to pull off the lid.

"That's nothing," Ana hastily said. She quickly explained about the Hudsons' Valentine's Day bash that would take place the following evening.

"Holy cow!" Emma exclaimed, fluffing back the tissue to see the dress inside. "That's not nothing."

"I'm sending it back," Ana rushed to explain.

"Why on earth would you send this back?" Emma pulled the dress from the box. Yards and yards of ocean-blue chiffon fluttered to the floor.

Ana, who hadn't seen the dress until now, nearly gasped. She recognized the fabric before Emma had even pulled it from the box. She was intimately acquainted with the dress.

"Never mind that," Emma kept talking, apparently in conversation with herself. She held the dress up, admiring it. "Forget where it came from. How could you afford it?"

"I couldn't," Ana said grimly. "It's from Ward."

Emma's eyebrows shot up. "From Ward?" She drew the question out so that it was obvious she was asking about far more than merely the dress.

"Yes, from Ward," Ana repeated.

"And he's sending you clothes…why, precisely?"

Beneath Emma's inquisitive gaze, Ana remained steadfastly silent.

"Oh, come on," Emma protested. "You've got to give me something to go on! Taking you to the Hudsons' party for work, I could buy that. But why is he sending you clothes? Are you dating?"

"Sort of. I don't know." Ana gave a frustrated tug at a lock of hair. Explaining her relationship with Ward was far too complicated. Besides which, she was pretty sure Emma would not approve of her plan to have a quick fling with Ward. She gestured toward the dress Emma still held. "So I don't know what to think about this, damn it."

Emma smiled smugly. "When a man sends me a generous gift, I rarely curse him for it."

"It's not the generosity that I have a problem with. It's the dress itself that…"

She swallowed her curse of frustration, choosing instead to snatch the dress out of Emma's hand. Some tiny part of her just wanted to rip the thing to shreds. But she didn't dare. After all she'd worked too hard on it.

"I made this dress!" She shook it, the gossamer fabric cascading from her hand.

"What?" Emma asked.

"The last movie I worked on." She'd slaved over the dress, over several versions of it actually.

"That sword and sandals epic?"

"Exactly. This is the dress the female lead wore in the big finale when she was about to be sacrificed to Scylla."

"Oh." Emma's eyes widened and then her brow furrowed into a frown. She moved closer to give the gown a better look. "How did Ward get it?"

"I have no idea." With a sigh, she unclenched her hand from the delicate fabric and studied the dress. As fitted the story line, the gown was Grecian in style, all flowing fabric and delicate tucks. Rhinestones had been sewn on to the wide strap that draped over one shoulder. Though Ana was curvier than the actress who'd worn the dress originally, the other woman had some help in the chest department and the dress was loose about the hips, so the dress should easily fit her.

Emma ran her hand over the gleaming stones. "I didn't know they had BeDazzlers in ancient Greece."

"They didn't have horrible sea monsters either. I don't think they were striving for authenticity." She shook her head. "I can't imagine how he got ahold of it."

"Ward does have a lot of connections." Emma stood beside her to study the gown. Then she gave Ana a knowing smile. "But he must have gone to a lot of trouble to find it. Especially at such short notice."

"Exactly." That was what made her so uncomfortable. When she'd made the quip about regretting that she'd never had the chance to wear one of her creations, she'd never dreamed he'd go to these incredible lengths to let her live out that fantasy.

"Why does that bother you?" Emma asked.

She held up the dress again, struggling to put her concerns into words. "It's a dress designed for a goddess. Literally. Don't you think I'm a little ordinary for a dress like this?"

"You are a lot of things, my friend, but ordinary is not one of them." Emma bumped her shoulder playfully against Ana's.

"Don't you think it's a little—" Ana broke off, searching for the right word. "I don't know. Extravagant?"

At this, Emma's smile grew broad and self-satisfied. "Not at all. Chase said that Ward is very romantic. That when he was dating Cara, he did all kinds of crazy grand gestures for her. Why do you think he wrote so many songs for her?"

Hearing it put like that, all of the anxiety that had been brewing in Ana's stomach coalesced into a tight ball of dread. She had expected their relationship to be all passionate sex. Instead, he was taking her on romantic dates and buying her presents. How was she supposed to stay emotionally uninvolved under these circumstances?

She forced a smile to cover her dread. Shaking the dress out with a flourish, she grabbed a hanger from the footstool by the bed. As she slipped the dress onto the hanger, she said cheerfully, "Well, if I'm going to this grand bash, I might as well make the most of it."

Emma's face blossomed with glee. She looked like she might very well have clapped her hands if her cast hadn't prevented her. "Okay, we'll need to start with a pedicure and manicure, then we'll need to figure out something for your hair. I'm thinking something Grecian and piled on top—"

"Hold on there, fairy godmother," Ana interrupted, as she propped open the door to her wardrobe and hung the dress from the edge. "I can handle that all on my own tomorrow afternoon after your wedding. And you're the one getting married tomorrow. What I meant was, if I'm going to be hobnobbing with the rich and famous, I might as well find a way to drum up some interest in Hannah's Hope."

Emma's expression went from excited to crestfallen. "Most people would sell their left foot to go to a party like this. On the arm of Ward Miller no less! And all you see is a chance to shill Hannah's Hope? Do you ever stop working?"

"Nope," Ana answered with a cheerful grin. "Can't afford to. Too much work to do." Then she jabbed Emma delicately in the ribs. "And admit it. If you were in my shoes, you'd do the same."

Emma gave a good-natured grumble. "Would not."

"Yeah, you would."

Emma ignored her. "Well, for now you should concentrate on just meeting people and talking about Hannah's Hope. Put out feelers. Maybe someone will be interested in coming to the street fair. Or…" Emma's eyes lit up as she paused dramatically. "We could invite them all to a gala fundraiser."

"Are we having a gala fundraiser?" Ana asked hesitantly.

"Well, we haven't planned one yet." Emma all but bubbled as she warmed to the idea. "But we should! Think about it. It just makes sense. You can talk up Hannah's Hope tomorrow night at this Valentine's Day thing. Ward can invite all the bigwigs he knows. Chase can, too, for that matter. We can host the event in a couple of months when we have some real successes to show off and—"

"How is Rafe going to feel about this?"

Emma's gaze narrowed in fierce protectiveness. "Right now, I'm so not concerned about how Rafe feels about anything."

"Oookay." Apparently, Emma was still worried that Rafe planned to dismantle the company bit by bit. Ana knew Chase was doing everything in his power to convince Rafe to take a different approach, but if Emma's reaction was any indication, he must not be making very much progress. Over drinks, Emma had mentioned that she'd done what she could to smooth over the rift between the stepbrothers, but apparently, her generosity of spirit extended only so far.

"Just think about it," Emma continued. "You've been worried about funding anyway. This is the perfect way to secure funding for the charity."

Ana was warming to the idea. "I don't think anyone at Hannah's Hope has the experience to organize something like this. Well, maybe you do." She dropped her gaze to Emma's belly. "But you're going to have your hands full in the coming months. We're going to have to hire someone to plan it."

"Didn't you say you'd recently been to a wedding where you were really impressed by the party planner?" Emma asked.

"Yes, I did." She gave her temple a quick tap, trying to pull up the woman's name. "She was just starting her own business and looking for work. She would be perfect for the job. Paige something. Adams maybe."

Emma smiled triumphantly. "If she's looking for work, this will be a dream job."

"I'll give her a call," Ana agreed. "But first we should put out some feelers. See what the rest of the staff thinks."

Emma, never one to give up a fight easily, reached over to finger the dress. "And the dress?"

"I'll think about it."

In fact, she was afraid she'd think about little else.

As they finished talking about the fundraiser, Ana gave the fabric of the dress one last touch. It was as light and airy as dragonfly wings.

Then she led Emma from the room and resolutely shut the door on the dress. She didn't want Emma to know how heartsick the sight of it made her.

She just didn't know how to feel about this new twist their relationship was taking. The Valentine's Day party, the dress... it all seemed so intimate.

Emma wouldn't understand. But then, Emma didn't know about Cara's sunglasses.

Nine

When she didn't say anything about the dress, Ward wondered if she would wear it. So he was pleased when he stopped by her house to pick her up and found her dressed in it. She looked exactly as he'd imagined. And, yes, he'd even imagined the frown.

"I'm glad you wore the dress," he said, leaning in to brush a quick kiss across her cheek. Of course, he'd seen her at the wedding just that morning. At the time it had been all he could do not to pull her fully into his arms and stake his claim on her where everyone could see. But he was trying to respect her wishes to keep things quiet.

Besides, stirring up gossip wasn't the best idea at someone else's wedding, when everyone was supposed to be focusing on the bride. The ceremony had been simple, yet lovely, as elegant as the bride herself. Ana had cried openly during the ceremony and the small reception that followed. Though he'd been curious about her parents, who'd also attended, he'd stayed firmly on the groom's side of the celebration, well away from temptation.

Even now, he had to force himself to put some distance between them.

Her frown deepened for an instant. "How did you even know about the dress?"

"I asked CeCe."

"This wasn't a Hudson Pictures movie. I've never worked for them."

"True, but CeCe grew up in Hollywood. She knows everyone. She told me this was the most gorgeous dress she'd ever seen. She said this was the dress you'd want to wear at least once, even if you'd worked your fingers to bloody nubs sewing it."

"Well, at least she has excellent taste." Ana smiled a bit reluctantly. "And I'm glad you followed my advice and didn't rent a limo."

He guided her down toward his Lexus. "It's an hour and half drive into Beverly Hills. If we were alone in the back of a limo, I couldn't promise to keep my hands to myself."

Ana didn't know what she expected from the Hudsons' bash. Obscene displays of wealth. Check. Obnoxious paparazzi. Check—though they were barred at the door. A dazzling array of stars. Check.

What she had not expected was to be blindly welcomed into their midst. As a costume designer, she'd mostly lingered on the fringes of Hollywood society. Tonight she was escorted into its upper echelons.

The Hudsons' annual bash was held at Hudson Manor, a sprawling Elizabethan mansion that ate up acres and acres of prime Beverly Hills real estate. The entire first floor of the manor had been lavishly decorated in red hearts and pink ribbons. The kitschy decorations contrasted sharply with the elegant surroundings.

Ward fit right in among all the stars and seemed to know nearly everyone. She did her part to talk up Hannah's Hope to anyone who displayed even the tiniest smidge of interest and she had several people who seemed genuinely intrigued. She found she was better at the schmoozing than she thought she'd be.

But she was nowhere near as good at it as Ward was. Listening to him talk up Hannah's Hope was almost as impressive as watching him play on stage. He was a genius. And his passionate enthusiasm for Hannah's Hope only made her feel more vulnerable. Why couldn't Ward be shallow and self-serving?

Ana excused herself to find the bathroom while Ward was chatting with the star of a late-night show. As she left the bathroom, she ran into CeCe Hudson. Ana was surprised that the other woman even remembered her. Yes, they'd met only about an hour before, but surely she was just a face in the crowd of hundreds.

"How are you enjoying the party?" the petite brunette asked.

"It's wonderful," Ana enthused.

CeCe chuckled. "Liar. You're miserable."

"I—" Ana stammered.

"Don't worry. I won't tell anyone." CeCe linked her arm through Ana's and started to guide her toward the buffet. "I used to hate these kinds of things, too. But it goes with the territory, right? You date someone rich and powerful, you end up hanging out with the shallow and the vain."

"I—" Ana fumbled for a response. Finally, she settled on, "Ward and I aren't dating."

CeCe slanted an assessing look at Ana. "Really?" She didn't sound in the least bit convinced.

"Really. I'm only here to promote Hannah's Hope."

CeCe arched an eyebrow. "Naturally. Jack mentioned the benefit you're thinking of throwing. Great idea, by the way." They'd reached the buffet table and CeCe picked up a plate and pushed it into Ana's hands. "Be sure to let me know if Hudson Pictures can do anything."

"Thank you. That's very generous."

"Ward's a good guy. It's the least we can do for the woman he's not dating."

"We're really not—"

But CeCe cut her off. "Hey, I'm all in favor of keeping things out of the press. Reporters can muck up anything, can't they?"

"That's certainly true," Ana agreed. The press had a way of sticking their collective noses in at precisely the wrong time.

On the way into the party, they'd badgered Ward about whether or not he was returning to a musical career. They'd asked about the studio work he'd been doing and every time he'd tried to steer the conversation back to an up-and-coming musician whose album Ward was producing, they'd changed the subject. Nor did they let him talk much about Hannah's Hope. Apparently, the media heard only what they wanted to hear.

The reporters' persistence didn't seem to bother Ward at all. He seemed oblivious to how invasive their questions were. Throughout the ordeal, he was as charming and relaxed as he was…well, at a party.

Almost as if she could read her thoughts, CeCe gave a little cringe. "Sorry about all the reporters outside the party. It used to be the Hudsons never allowed that. But now that we're raising money for breast cancer research, we figure any press for the cause is a good thing. Besides, some people give more generously when it's going to be on *Entertainment Tonight*."

Ana and CeCe chatted for several minutes as they worked their way through the buffet line. Ana felt marginally more comfortable, but eventually, CeCe's hostessing duties took her away and Ana was left on her own again.

She made her way back to Ward. Unfortunately, when she rounded the corner, she saw him talking to the one person she least expected. Ridley Sinclair. The supposed happily married star who had hit on her and then made her work life miserable.

Ridley Sinclair was a first-rate jerk. Her last job had been one misery after another because he was always on set. After all, his wife had been the star of the movie.

Ana never wanted to see him again. Yet, here they were. At the same party. And he was talking to Ward. And here she was, in the dress that had been made for his wife.

Annoyed, she ducked aside, standing on the outskirts of a nearby cluster of people, hoping to wait out the conversation before returning to Ward's side. She didn't intend to eavesdrop, but she could still hear their conversation.

"Hey, I noticed you were here with that costume designer," Ridley slurred.

Ana gave a sidewise glance. Ward and Ridley were standing with their backs to her. They'd have to turn completely around to see her. She nearly left, but wanted to be nearby so she could sneak back to Ward's side as soon as Ridley left.

Ridley held a drink in his hand, gesturing broadly and splashing the amber liquid. She wasn't surprised that he was already drunk so early in the evening. What a jerk. How had she ever imagined Ward might be even remotely similar to him?

"What's her name? Amanda something, right?" Ridley was asking.

"Ana," Ward answered, his voice tight.

Ridley seemed not to hear the note of warning in Ward's voice, because he kept talking. "Yeah. Ana. She worked on my last movie."

The guy had maybe ten lines. He'd been cast only because his wife wanted him in it. And suddenly it was *his* movie. Ana smirked to herself. Thank God she didn't have to deal with him anymore.

She should have walked away then. And nearly did. Ward could obviously fend for himself.

But then Ridley was saying, "Man, she is one tight little piece of—"

She was about one syllable away from socking the guy in the jaw herself, when Ward interrupted him.

"I wouldn't finish that sentence if I were you," Ward said smoothly. His voice was calm. Completely rational. Containing none of the blustering indignation her own set-down would have.

She stilled, listening intently, but trying to hide it behind sipping her drink.

"What?" Ridley asked stupidly.

"I suggest," Ward said politely, "that you speak about Ms. Rodriguez with more respect."

"Or what?" Ridley scoffed.

"I have a lot of friends in Hollywood, Mr. Sinclair. Probably more than you do. Despite your wife's success. Now, if you'll excuse me."

Ward left Ridley standing alone. The idiot seemed to have barely realized he'd just been threatened.

Ana slipped quietly away, all too aware of what had just happened. Ward had come to her defense. She hadn't needed him to. If Ridley Sinclair had had the balls to say those things to her face, she would have socked him in the jaw. But he hadn't. He'd said them to Ward. And Ward had stepped up to defend her. He'd calmly and effectively threatened the man's career. For her.

She'd never wanted anyone to rush to her rescue. Had never needed that before. Somehow Ward's behavior completely disarmed her. She dashed back down the hall leading to the bathroom. Finding herself suddenly alone, she leaned against the wall and pressed a hand to her stomach.

She hadn't wanted to come to this stupid Valentine's Day ball in the first place. She hadn't wanted the dress. She hadn't wanted the romance. And the last thing she needed was some romantic hero to sweep her off her feet.

No, her feet needed to stay firmly planted on the ground. If she stayed here at this party. Wearing this dress. With Ward here to gallantly come to her rescue. He wasn't even going to have to sweep her off her feet. She was very much afraid her feet were going to float right off the ground.

After ditching Ridley Sinclair, Ward searched for Ana for several minutes before stumbling upon Jack, who he'd been hoping to find alone for most of the evening. Ward pulled him aside. After talking for a while, he quietly slipped an envelope into Jack's hand, glad there was no one around to see the exchange. He'd made the check out directly to Jack, with the understanding that his friend would quietly shuffle the funds over to the charity. Every year he made a donation and every year Jack argued with him about it. But this was the first year he'd been able to do it in person.

Jack accepted the check without looking at it. "Are you sure you don't want a receipt for your tax records?"

"If I wanted a receipt, then it would no longer be an anonymous donation, now, would it?"

"Good point." Jack tucked the envelope into the interior pocket of his tuxedo jacket. "And since you seem determined that people not find out that you donate money to a good cause, who am I to dissuade you?"

They both knew the real reason Ward wanted the donation to be anonymous. Cara had been obsessed with distancing herself from any of the cancer charities. She'd been terrified of having her life's work overshadowed by her death and had made Ward promise not to besmirch her legacy. He honored her memory by never letting the media know when he donated to the causes she'd so stubbornly ignored.

Before Jack could press the issue, CeCe walked up. Jack instantly pulled CeCe to his side. CeCe slipped her hand onto Jack's chest with an easy familiarity that made something ache deep inside of Ward. He remembered, just barely, what it had been like to be as relaxed with another person. As comfortable.

But it had been a long time since he'd felt that. And even then, it had been more illusion than reality.

To distract Jack from the issue of the check—or perhaps to distract himself—Ward asked, "So where'd you ditch my date?"

"Ana?" CeCe asked with a frown. "Actually, she's why I came over. She and I talked for a while, but as soon as I left her alone for a minute, I saw her heading for the door. Racing, practically. I think she must have seen someone she didn't like."

Ward smothered a curse of frustration and immediately excused himself. He hoped to catch up with Ana, but by the time he made it out to the valet stand, she was already gone. The attendant told him that a cab had dropped someone off just as she was rushing out.

Ward sent the man off in search of the Lexus and stood there alone, fuming. He'd left her alone for ten, maybe fifteen minutes. And she'd ditched him.

* * *

Ana balked when she heard how much a cab ride from L.A. to Vista del Mar would cost this time of night. She might have been better off renting a car, if any car rental places had been open. She briefly considered getting a hotel room, but just now, she longed for the simple familiarity of home even if it was a house she hadn't lived in long. With the taxi and the rental out of the question, she fell back on the reliable transportation of her youth. Public transportation.

Of course, taking the bus in a thousand-dollar evening gown was like begging to be mugged. So she had the cab drop her at a twenty-four-hour discount store, where she bought the cheapest sweater and pair of jeans she could find and a roomy bag in which she could carry the dress, neatly rolled up. She changed in the bathroom and used a damp paper towel to wipe off most of her makeup. Then she caught the bus to Union Station. Thank God for the ten-thirty train to San Diego. From there it was just a short bus ride back up to Vista del Mar. Still, it was after one by the time the taxi dropped her off in front of her house.

Climbing out of the cab, she stilled as she saw Ward's Lexus parked in front of her house. The fact that it was empty offered her no comfort. Especially not when a glance at the front door revealed him waiting for her there.

She fed the cabbie the fee.

He followed her gaze to her doorstep. "Hey, you okay? You know him?"

"Yes. Unfortunately, I do."

The cabbie frowned. "You want me to drop you somewhere else? I won't charge you any extra."

She smiled, trying to look reassuring, but pretty sure her smile looked sad instead. "No. He'd never hurt me." Not physically, anyway. Emotionally, that was a whole 'nother ball of wax. "I just didn't want to face him tonight, that's all."

The cabbie looked from her to Ward and then back again. "Hey, that isn't—"

"No, it's not." But she slipped the cabbie another twenty just to be sure he believed her.

He drove away, hopefully tipped into silence. She could only wish she were as easily satisfied. But of course, if money was all she needed to find happiness, this would all be much easier.

When she walked up the path to the door, Ward stood, blocking her way. "Where the hell have you been?"

She elbowed him aside as she pulled her keys from her beaded clutch. "Why does it matter?" she asked, as she slid the key into the lock. "You weren't interested in me being there at all. I was just a pretty accessory for you to have on your arm."

"That's not true," he growled.

"It is true." She stepped inside, knowing better than to try to keep him out. But of course, it wasn't true. Not even close. She wished it had been true. She wished that he'd treated her badly, because then at least she'd have a legitimate reason to be furious with him. As it was, she could hardly criticize him for being too charming. Too protective.

She would sound like a crazy woman. And she was starting to wonder if that wasn't too close to the truth.

She dropped the bag containing the dress on the floor by the front door, too exhausted to hang up the dress and care for it as it deserved. She sank to the edge of the sofa.

She'd had plenty of time to think on the long train ride home. It was a trip she was all too familiar with after her years working in L.A. when she'd made frequent trips home to visit her family and Emma. There was something soothingly familiar about taking public transportation.

It was such a nice reminder of what her life was all about. Helping people who'd had fewer advantages than she'd had. Hard work. Making a difference. Those were the things that mattered.

She didn't need grand romantic gestures or fancy dresses.

"I didn't fit in with those people," she said, knowing that she was stretching for a viable explanation. "Look, it's late. I'm tired. I don't want to talk about this now."

If he pressed her for an explanation, she was afraid that she might end up telling him the truth. She was perilously close to falling in love with him.

* * *

Stifling his annoyance, Ward paced to the far side of the living room, rounding the end of the sofa. It helped him resist the urge to shake some sense into her. "I'm going to pretend you didn't just say that," he bit out. "We both know you're just grasping at straws trying to find some reason to be mad at me, when you know you're the one at fault here."

"I'm at fault?" she asked in outraged indignation.

"Yes. You're the one who walked out on me. And didn't answer your phone any of the fifteen times I called you."

"My—" she broke off in genuine confusion. "Oh. My phone. I put it in the bag with the dress." She shrugged. "I guess I didn't hear it ring."

"You *guess* you didn't hear it ring? For four hours? Do you have any idea how worried I was?"

She at least had the sense to look embarrassed, but it seemed to annoy her and she shrugged it off, casually saying, "I'm sorry."

He grabbed her by the arm and pulled her around so she faced him. "You're sorry? You pull a stupid, reckless stunt like that and the best you can come up with is 'I'm sorry'?"

She jerked her arm away from his hand. "Yes. I'm sorry you were worried. But the stunt was neither stupid nor reckless."

"Then where have you been for the past four hours?"

She arched an eyebrow. "Have you ever taken buses all over L.A. and then picked up the late-night train to San Diego? Public transportation is slow."

"How is riding buses and trains around L.A. in the middle of the night not stupid?"

"I've been riding buses and trains around L.A. since I was a child. I may talk and dress like a rich white girl most of the time, but I've been in and out of just as many poor neighborhoods as I have rich ones. I know how to handle myself."

"It may be true that you know how to handle yourself." He grabbed both her arms now and didn't let her go. When he spoke his voice was low and laden with all of his pent-up fears. "But

I don't know how to handle having you out there on your own without knowing that you're safe."

"Oh." Her brow furrowed in delightful confusion.

"Just—" He pulled her close, bumping his head against hers, relief that she was safe finally flooding through him. "Don't do that again."

"Okay." She nodded, seeming to melt against him. When she spoke, her voice sounded tight. "I didn't know you'd worry."

She sounded so genuinely confused, he couldn't rail against her again, even though he wanted to. He had to remind himself that she wasn't used to living in the limelight as he was. She could truly pick up a train in the middle of the night and no one would know or care. She could disappear in a crowd. Something he hadn't done in over twenty years.

"I really am sorry." Her words came out in a rush. "But that party, that just wasn't my thing. I can't imagine why you wanted me there."

"Why is it so hard for you to believe that I just wanted to be with you? That I just wanted to impress you?"

She threw up her hands in obvious frustration. "Because you're the most impressive person I've ever met." Her expression softened and she inched closer to him. "Without introducing me to famous people I don't care about. You and you alone are impressive." She reached for him then, twining her arms around his shoulders. "Your total dedication to CMF. Your amazing talent as a songwriter and musician. Those are the—"

He wrenched himself from her arms and turned away, unable to even look at her. Wishing he'd pulled away sooner, before she'd spoken of his amazing talent. And don't forget that dedication.

Right. His amazing dedication to a charity he didn't really believe in. In honor of a wife he'd failed miserably. And his amazing talent that hadn't meant jack when push came to shove. But it was nice to know that those were the qualities Ana most admired.

She must have read the tension in his posture, because she walked up and ran a hand along his back.

"Is it so hard for you to believe that none of that stuff matters to me? That when I want to be with you, it's with you alone. That I don't want to be with you in a crowd of people. I just want to be with you."

"We've been over this before. I can't be alone with you, without wanting to strip your clothes off and—"

But she interrupted him. "Then what are you waiting for?"

She didn't have to ask twice. She didn't really expect to. The words were barely out of her mouth before he'd pulled her to him and molded her body against his. His mouth was hot and hard over hers as the last of his anger melted into desire.

Yes, her entire being seemed to sing in response. *Finally, inevitably, yes.*

Every cell in her body seemed to call out to his. Her very blood pounded in rhythm with her need. This was what she wanted from him. What she needed. And if he just gave it to her, maybe her heart would forget all the stupid things it wanted.

His hands seemed everywhere at once, hot and needy. Slipping up under the edge of her shirt. Skimming over the backside of her jeans. Pulling her hips against his.

And everywhere he touched her, she was aware of the roughness of his fingertips. Of the mastery of his hands. Burning his mark onto her skin. Onto her very soul.

She trembled under his ministrations, all too aware of how clumsy she felt. How every aspect of this was new for her. And despite that, how right it felt to press her body against his. As if this was what she'd waited for all her life. As if this was what she was meant for.

She arched against him, unable to get close enough. To touch enough of him. And then he backed her up one step. And another. And another.

Finally, she realized his intention. Nodding toward the door, she wrenched her mouth from his. "Bedroom," she panted. "That way."

He didn't need to be told twice, but swept her up into his arms and carried her there, as smoothly and as easily as the heroes from the romantic movies she'd watched as a girl.

He kicked the door open with his foot and strode into the room, then laid her gently down on the bed. Her room was relentlessly feminine, with it's brightly colored quilt and sunny yellow throw pillows. Suddenly, she was aware that no man had ever been in this room. Not just this room, but any of her bedrooms.

But before she had a chance to feel self-conscious about that, he'd stepped back. She watched, fascinated as he stripped off his tuxedo jacket and let it drop on the floor. As he started on the shirt buttons, she rose up on her knees to help him. As each button slipped free, her pulse quickened and with it, her desire. She felt her blood roaring through her veins, her need thundering through her. Frustrated by his slow progress, she dropped her hands to his belt buckle. Her fingers trembled as she flicked it open, unfastened his pants and tugged his shirt free. She tugged the belt from his pants and then sat back on her heels to admire her handiwork.

Standing there before her, with his hair tousled and his shirt hanging open to reveal a narrow swath of skin, he looked like something from a fantasy. Or maybe an ad campaign for high-end cologne. In comparison to the other half-naked men she'd seen—entirely in a professional capacity—Ward's body was stunningly masculine. The hair on his chest was sparse and dark, his muscles defined without being sculpted. This was the body of a grown man, fully in his prime. As sexual as it was powerful. Able to protect and provide.

But it was the expression on his face that sent shivers of pleasure through her. He gazed at her with such intensity, such powerful longing that she knew she'd made the right choice. It was as simple and as powerful as this: she wanted him. Desperately. And for once, she was going to give herself what she wanted.

"Stop looking at me like that," Ward ordered, his voice rough with desire.

Ana's gaze darted to his. "Like what?" Her voice was breathy.

"Like I'm a five-course dessert." He flicked off his cuff links, letting them fall into his open palm and then pocketing them. Slowly, he shucked his shirt, letting it fall, unnoticed, to the floor.

He moved with precision and control. His expression taut and hungry, gazing into her eyes as if he had to cling tightly to the last shreds of his control or lose it completely.

Ten

Closing the distance between them, he cupped her cheek with one hand. With his other, Ward carefully plucked out the bobby pins holding back her hair. Once the silken waves were free, he brought them to his face and inhaled deeply, drinking in Ana's intoxicating scent. Then he poured all of that desperate need into his kiss. Her mouth was warm and inviting. A tempting buffet of textures and sensations.

There were so many things he wanted to say, so much emotion he needed to express. So many things he didn't even know how to tell her. All his life, he'd used words to seduce. But that only worked when he had a guitar in his hands. When he could coax out a melody to create the mood, to entice a woman into feeling what he wanted her to feel. Kissing Ana now, he felt vulnerable. Woefully inadequate. Barely up to the task of making love to her.

He had no way of knowing what was going on in that stubborn brain of hers. No way of judging if she wanted him with the same desperate neediness that he felt. All he knew was that he'd never felt this way before. Not even with Cara.

With Cara, everything had been right on the surface. There'd never been any deeper meaning, no hidden indecipherable emotions. No need to take things slowly. And no desperation.

With Ana, everything was different. More intense. And his innate talent with words failed him.

In the end, all he could do was worship her with his body. With reverent hands, he pulled her sweater up over her head. Her breasts were bare beneath it. Perfect. Lush and inviting. Begging to be kissed, lathed and lavished with attention. Which he did with complete devotion.

But still, the rest of her body beckoned, tempting him farther down. She shimmied out of her jeans and he quickly stripped her of her silken underwear. When he slipped his hand between her legs there was an instant of resistance before her thighs fell open to his touch. But once he eased open her lips, she was delightfully moist and hot enough to burn him. All but trembling with need, he dipped his fingers into her over and over again as his thumb found the nub of tender skin at her entrance. A groan pulled from low in her throat as she bucked on the bed. He felt her muscles clench around his fingers as the very first tremors of an orgasm coursed through her. He couldn't resist tasting her then, suckling the sweet honey of her arousal as he pushed her over the edge into oblivion.

Ana was trembling, drifting slowly back to earth, feeling as though all the molecules of her body had been scattered and were only now pulling themselves back together.

She was only vaguely aware that Ward's warmth had left her. She shoved herself up onto an elbow to watch as he stripped off his pants and boxers.

"Condoms," she said with a nod toward the bedside table, surprised by how breathless she sounded.

She'd bought them just last week. Her first ever condom purchase. Terrified she'd fumble and embarrass herself, she'd sat in her bathroom for an hour one evening practicing with a banana. Ward never gave her the chance to show off her fledgling skills, but rather extracted one from the package and quickly put it on. A moment later, he was above her again.

He thrust into her. Pain seared through her as her virginity was ripped away. She squeezed her eyes shut, sucking in a deep breath.

It hurt. Worse than she'd expected. Worse than the novels she'd read had led her to believe. She seemed stretched. Too full. But as she breathed out, slowly, the tightness eased.

Only then did she open her eyes. He'd stopped moving completely. His eyes were wide in an expression of surprised confusion that made her cheeks redden with embarrassment.

She squeezed her eyes closed again. So much for him not noticing.

"Ana," he gasped.

She forced herself to look up at him, taking in the grim set of his lips as he sucked shallow breaths.

"It's okay," she said.

"It's not."

She felt him pulling away from her. "Oh, no you don't," she ground out. The pain was nearly gone now and she brought her legs up to hook behind his buttocks. Twining her hands through his hair, she pulled up to press herself against him. She kissed him, pouring into it all of the things she should have said before, but hadn't. How much she wanted this. How much she wanted him. She'd been waiting for this her whole life.

Every other woman she'd known had carelessly tossed aside her virginity while still a teenager. But not her. She'd waited. Not just because she was pressured to succeed by her parents. That was the excuse she'd always given herself. But the truth was, deep in her heart, she'd been waiting. Waiting for him. Waiting for the man she loved.

She tried to say all of that with just her kiss. Either he understood her unspoken message or his restraint finally snapped. Because slowly, as if he were fighting it with every fiber of his being, he began moving again. He slipped his hand down between her legs and began stroking her again, slowly edging her closer to another climax. The pressure inside of her built. The burning need to be full of him, finally met.

By the time he thrust into her one last time—his head thrown back, her name a prayer on his lips—she was right there with him as pleasure rocketed through her body.

Ana had heard plenty of her friends complain about their boyfriends and husbands falling asleep immediately after sex. It wasn't a good sign that she was hoping Ward would follow in the footsteps of his maligned gender and do the same.

He didn't keep her in suspense for long, but almost immediately rolled off her, to sit on the side of the bed, his elbows propped on his knees and his head in his hands. She pulled the sheet up almost to her chin and then laid there, heart pounding, waiting for him to say something. Anything.

As a girl, she used to fantasize about this moment. About giving herself to the man she loved. It always involved him loving her back. For years now, she'd told herself that she hadn't been saving her virginity for any particular reason. That it was more inconvenience than anything else. But the flood of emotions she'd felt just now showed that particular disillusion for the lie it was. Though she hadn't actually had time for her fantasies to catch up with her emotions, she didn't exactly need Dr. Phil here to tell her this was not going to play out like some schoolgirl dream.

Even if she hadn't already known the truth about Cara and those damn sunglasses, one didn't need a lot of experience to know that a man who'd just had sex with a woman he loved wouldn't sit on the side of the bed, head in hands as if he were miserable. No, these were the actions of a man racked with guilt. A man who—dear God—was ashamed of his actions.

Which meant in his eyes, she'd just gone from a desired woman to a burden.

Crap, crap and double crap.

How was she going to fix this?

Ward had had sex with a lot of women over the years, but not a damn one of them had been a virgin. Until now.

Didn't it just figure that Ana would be the one to slip past his defenses?

His mind raced, reviewing every moment of their time together, looking for clues. At times, she'd seemed so worldly. So confident and savvy. She'd worked in Hollywood, for goodness' sake. How did a beautiful, sexy woman like her work in Hollywood—where sex was practically a currency—and stay a virgin?

But of course, she hadn't *stayed* in Hollywood, had she? Maybe that should have been his number one clue. But he never suspected that she was a virgin. And she'd never told him. Damn it.

He didn't know who he was madder at. Himself for not guessing or her for not telling him.

He was still debating that point, when he felt her roll to her side and reach out a hand toward him. "Ward—" she began.

He shot to his feet. "No," he said instinctively. Though what exactly he was protesting, he couldn't say. Maybe the whole damn situation. He searched the floor for his boxers and pants and quickly pulled them on.

His shirt lay on the floor a few feet away and he went to retrieve it.

"Ward—" she called again, the distress in her voice more apparent now. "Don't go!"

He paused in the act of bending down to pick up the shirt. Christ, did she really think he was going to walk out on her without even talking about this? What kind of selfish SOB did she think he was?

He swiped the shirt off the floor and shrugged into it as he strode back to the bed. She'd risen onto her knees and still held the white sheet clutched to her chest. Her hair was loose about her shoulders, a luxuriant tumble of dark waves. She couldn't have looked more exotically sexual if she'd been posed for a photo shoot. The image was all the more enticing because he knew she was naked beneath that sheet. Because he now knew every luscious curve of her body, every fragrant hollow, every sensitive valley.

He tried to pull his attention away from her and button his

shirt, but he couldn't pull his gaze from her and the buttons kept slipping out of his fingers. Sitting like that, she looked fit for a pinup poster.

And she was a virgin. Or rather, she had been.

Apparently, his brain could handle only one complex task at a time, and deciphering the motives of one obstinate female was taxing his limited abilities. He gave up on the buttons and thrust his hand through his hair instead.

Finally, he forced out the question that was choking him. "Why didn't you say anything?"

She blinked, either surprised by his query or by the fact that he was still there. "About…" It seemed like the word was on the tip of her tongue, but she pulled it back, finishing with mulish stubbornness. "About what?"

So, she was going to force him to say it. Did she really think there was any chance he'd missed the obvious? Of course, he had missed all the signs of the obvious. Or misread them.

"About. Being. A virgin." He bit out the words not bothering to keep his frustration from his voice.

Her chin bumped up defiantly and when she spoke her clipped tone echoed his. "Because, it wasn't a big deal."

"Not a big—" He broke off, ran a hand through his hair. Again. And sucked in a deep breath. Again. And tried to speak more calmly. Again. "You were a virgin. You'd never had sex before. Ever. There's no way that's not a big deal."

He studied her expression as he spoke, taking in every nuance of her expression. He saw the uncertainty that flickered across her face. The moment of doubt. Saw her mustering her defenses. And even saw what might have been a faint sheen of tears before she blinked them away.

"Christ, Ana, I'm—"

"Don't you dare say you're sorry," she ordered, whatever vulnerability he'd seen in her gaze was instantly gone. She climbed from the bed, giving the sheet a vicious tug to free it from the bottom of the bed so it came with her.

How the hell was he supposed to respond to that?

She didn't give him much of a chance to reply, but carefully draped the sheet around her body and stalked off toward the bathroom. He made a step to follow her, only to find the door soundly slammed in his face.

He scanned the room in which he'd been left alone. He hadn't exactly been in the mood to notice the decor before now. Art deco–style furniture—the kind that could be bought inexpensively at antique stores—had been sanded down and painted a funky bold palette of sunny-yellow, lime-green and bright turquoise. There was a headboard, a dresser and a wardrobe. The linens were a creamy white with colorful throws. The overall effect was somehow a perfect reflection of her personality. Bright, determined, with a depth and complexity that stemmed from its very simplicity.

The one thing he didn't see was a closet door. Which meant it was probably on the other side of the bathroom. She'd have the chance to get dressed, as well as time to leap to all sorts of conclusions about his emotional state.

He crossed to the door and rapped his knuckles on the door frame. "Come on out, Ana."

There was no response.

"We need to talk about this."

Again, there wasn't the faintest rumble of an answer.

His frustration ratcheted up by several degrees. "You might as well come out, because I'm not leaving. Not until we talk about this, damn it."

He bit back the string of curses he wanted to hurl at the offending door. He wanted to kick the damn thing. Or better yet, to kick it down. But what he really wanted to do was apologize. Which she'd ordered him not to do.

But of course he was sorry. But at the same time, he'd experienced exquisite pleasure in her arms. So was he sorry he'd made love to her? No. And he didn't exactly regret the fact that she'd been a virgin. The opposite in fact. The thought of her being with another man filled him with a primitive and very uncivilized rage. So, no, he wasn't sorry about that, either.

He just wished…

He sank to the edge of the bed as a realization washed over

him. He wished she'd told him herself. He wished it had been a big deal to her. Because it sure as hell had been a big deal to him.

Even without knowing she was a virgin, making love to Ana had been a big deal to him. Hell, this was the first time he felt like he had been *making love* to a woman since Cara had died.

That summed it up perfectly.

He'd had sex with women since Cara. But he hadn't made love. He hadn't really cared about any of those other women. He hadn't felt so much as a scrap of real emotion until Ana.

And that was the way he'd wanted it. Cara's death had been brutal on him. Worse, still, was the way she'd pulled away from him. From the moment she'd been diagnosed, she'd started pushing him away. Suddenly, the woman with whom he'd once shared everything couldn't even talk to him about the disease that was tearing her apart. Even in the beginning, when her prognosis was good, she'd distanced herself. Thrown herself into her charitable works. She'd given so much of herself to others, there was nothing left for him.

Talk about a complaint you can't even voice aloud. What kind of jerk complains because his dying wife is spending too much time helping the needy children of the world? At first, he'd thought it was because she feared not accomplishing all the things she wanted to in life. For a long time he wondered if she just couldn't stand to be close to anyone. By the end of her life, he realized the truth. She'd fallen in love with a rock star and ended up married to a mere human. She just didn't want to spend her dying days with someone who'd been such a disappointment.

Not that she'd ever said so much aloud, but he'd felt her emotional distance like a third person in the room with them every time he'd been with her. On her deathbed, every conversation they'd had had been about what she hadn't yet accomplished in her charitable works.

It was why he'd started the Cara Miller Foundation. He couldn't be what she'd needed when she was alive, but he could damn well fulfill her dying wish.

Of course, this was a hell of time to remember all of this. But this was a hell of a situation to be in.

Cara—the love of his life—had pushed him away. And now he was involved with yet another stubborn woman determined to keep her emotional distance. So here he was. Right where he'd sworn he'd never be again.

The funny thing was he'd spent so much time trying to protect Ana from himself, he never wondered who was going to protect him from her.

He was well on his way to falling in love with her, and she… well, who the hell knew what she felt for him.

What exactly was he supposed to say here? *I wanted it to be a big deal. I wanted you to care more about me. Why do you think I waited to sleep with you…? I waited because I wanted it to matter. I wanted you to care.*

Yeah. That would sound about as manly as a thirteen-year-old girl. Hell, actual thirteen-year-old girls sounded tougher than that. At least the ones he knew did.

If he said anything even approaching that, it would send Ana running for the door. If she hadn't already been walking in that direction anyway.

Eleven

Before Ward could even consider how to handle this, the bathroom door opened.

She'd pulled her hair back off her face with a clip and scrubbed off the last traces of her makeup. She'd dressed once again in jeans and a sweater, but this time they weren't clothes she'd bought God only knew where. They were her own clothes, obviously favorites. The jeans flattered Ana's curves, the sweater was conservative, hiding as much as it revealed, only hinting at the bounty beneath.

Looking at her now, it seemed so obvious she'd been a virgin. As inherently sensual as she was, she kept that part of herself tightly under wraps. Hidden under layers of prickly defenses and steely determination.

Whatever emotions she'd been wrestling with when she'd stormed off into the bathroom were now tightly under control. She looked very much as she had the first day they'd met. Wary. Reserved.

She gave him a quick once-over, judging his emotional state more quickly than he'd judged hers.

Her expression shifted to exasperated, as if she'd just read every thought that had passed through his mind while she was dressing and then dismissed them as being tiresome.

"Stop torturing yourself," she muttered, walking past him and out of the bedroom.

"Torturing myself?" he asked, following her.

She marched straight to the kitchen. "Yes. Obviously you've been playing it over and over again in your mind, trying to figure out what you should have done differently. Or maybe telling yourself how you should have guessed. Or—"

"Enough." He reached out for her arm, spinning her around to face him as he cut her off. So far, she was right on target and as whiny as he sounded in his own mind, he sure didn't need to hear her voice his doubts aloud. "If you think you know me so well, then you should understand exactly why I'm…what was the word you used? Oh, right, torturing myself."

"Honestly, though, I don't." For a moment, genuine confusion flickered across her face, then she shrugged. "I guess I didn't think you'd notice."

"Trust me, that's the kind of thing a guy notices. How could you imagine otherwise?"

Again she gave a little shrug, this one seeming almost self-effacing. "With all the women you've been with, and all the experience you have, I just thought…" She let her words trail off, leaving him to draw his own conclusions.

"That I was such a self-indulging wastrel that I wouldn't notice your virginity?"

"No! I just—"

"Thought I was too self-absorbed? Too selfish? Too what?" His anger grew with each question until he was looming over her, glaring down at her upturned face.

She met his gaze defiantly. "Why are you so sure this is all about you? It was my virginity. Why can't you just accept that if it's not a big deal for me that it shouldn't be a big deal for you, either?"

"Because I can't."

"Why?" Her chin bumped up and her gaze narrowed in determination. This time it was her stepping closer to him. "What would you have done differently if you'd known? What would you have changed?"

"I..." But before he had a chance to think of an answer, she continued, getting right in his face.

"Would you have been more sensitive?" she continued. All signs of the nervous virgin had vanished. Or maybe that had merely been a figment of his imagination, anyway. "Would you have been more attentive to my needs? Would you have made sure I climaxed three or four times, instead of merely twice?"

"That's enough," he all but growled out, his own temper rising to match hers. Her flippant tone was driving him crazy.

She arched a haughty brow. "Or what?"

"Let's not go there." He stepped away from her before he did something he regretted, like pull her back into his arms and make love to her all over again. Which would so not be helpful right now, even though the tension between them was still simmering.

"Look," she began again, her tone marginally softer. "I never meant to deceive you."

"Then what was it you did want?"

"I just didn't want it to be a big deal." She spoke slowly, enunciating each word.

"But it is. You were a virgin. At... How old are you? Twenty-six? Twenty-seven?"

"Twenty-seven," she muttered, suddenly unable to meet his gaze. As if her age were something to apologize for.

"Nobody's a virgin at twenty-seven by accident. Certainly no one who's as beautiful and vivacious as you."

Again, that defiance flashed in her eyes. As if his words were insults rather than compliments.

"How I look doesn't have anything to do with it. It's not as if I didn't have opportunity."

"That's precisely my point."

"It's just the way I was raised. That's all." She spun away from him, stalking to the other side of the room to stare out the window. "From the time I was twelve, my mother drilled it into my head. I couldn't mess around with boys. I couldn't sleep with them. I couldn't even date them. If I fell in love with some boy, and fooled around or had sex, I'd just end up pregnant and married by the time I was twenty. Just like almost every other poor Latina girl in Southern California."

Though her back was to him as she stared out the window into the darkness of the neighborhood, he could see the tension in the lines of her back. He could hear it in her voice, like she was quoting a lecture she'd heard over and over again, complete with hand gestures slicing through the air.

"If I got pregnant by twenty, it was all over. I'd be dooming myself to a life of poverty. The only way out was to stay out of trouble. Finish my education. Start my career. By the time I accomplished my goals and got a job out in L.A., I realized I was the oldest virgin in the city. And then there I was. Twenty-three, working in Hollywood, this beautiful and vivacious woman—" she practically sneered the words "—and every guy I dated expected me to be sexually experienced. Men were actually insulted if I didn't fall into bed with them on the first date."

There was enough bitterness in her tone for him to know there was more to that story.

"What is it you're not telling me?" He almost didn't want to know.

She shot him a surprised look. "It was nothing."

"Is it nothing the same way your virginity was nothing?" Her jaw tightened and her cheeks flushed. "Yeah," he continued. "That's what I thought. Why don't you tell me anyway and I'll be the judge of whether it was really nothing."

"Just the occasional actor who made things awkward when I didn't jump into bed with them."

"Who?" he bit out the question.

"Does that really matter?" Her tone sounded beleaguered.

"It matters." How was he going to hunt down the bastard and kill him if he didn't have a name? "Who was it?"

She studied his expression, her gaze narrowed and assessing. "You're not going to let this go, are you?"

"I'll let it go when you tell me who it was."

"Ridley Sinclair."

Ward immediately swore. Christ, he'd been talking to the guy just a few hours ago. Ridley Sinclair, who was supposedly happily married to the love of his life. And now he was finding out the guy was a cheating bastard. Who'd made Ana's life difficult.

"I'm going to kill him," Ward muttered.

Ana flashed an exasperated smile. "Please don't."

"He's why you left Hollywood," he surmised, piecing together another complicated swath of the puzzle.

"Not the only reason." Indignation laced her voice.

"So there were other men who harassed you?"

"It's not important!" she insisted. Again. "What's important is that I now have a job I love. A job I care about and where I can make a difference. I'm just desperate to make it work. That's what matters."

But despite all her protests, he could tell she still felt the sting of Sinclair's behavior. And as a result, she still didn't trust Ward entirely. Maybe she never would. But he understood her better now. Christ, no wonder Ana had freaked out last night and left the party. She must have overheard Sinclair's slurs.

He crossed to where she stood and pulled her gently to his chest. "I'm sorry."

She pulled away just enough to rest her palm against his cheek. "It's not your fault."

"Maybe not. But I was the one who dragged you to that party."

"Hey." Her tone was a little defensive, a little accusatory. "I could have said no."

"I made it pretty hard for you to say no," he countered.

"And I still make my own decisions."

Boy, that was the truth. He'd never met a more bullheaded woman. Still, he sensed there was something she wasn't saying. Something she didn't want him to know.

"If I really didn't want to go, I wouldn't have gone." Her voice wavered. "I just didn't expect it to be so hard."

He tipped her chin up forcing her to meet his gaze. "Well,

next time something is hard for you, talk to me about it instead of just leaving. You're not alone in this relationship."

"Is that was this is? A relationship?" Her voice caught. For once, Ana seemed…timid almost. Unsure of herself.

He didn't know which and didn't want to push the matter. Neither emotion was the giddy, joyful, postcoital rush of love he wished she was experiencing.

"Yes," he said firmly. Whatever doubts she'd been having, he wanted to banish them.

After a moment, she nodded. "Okay."

Then she pressed her body closer to his. Pushing up onto her toes, she pulled his head down to hers for a kiss that seared his very soul. Instantly, he felt himself harden again, which shocked the hell out of him. He'd just had her. It was inconceivable that he would want her again so soon. Not to mention impractical. His knowledge of virgins was fairly limited, but he didn't think she'd be up for a second round any time tonight.

After giving himself a moment to relish the feel of her against him, he extracted himself from her and set her firmly aside. He let his hand trail down her arm. "We'll pick this up in another day or two."

"But—"

"No arguing about this," he interrupted her. "You don't get to have everything your way."

She frowned, but gave a reluctant nod.

"I want to see you later today. After we've both gotten some sleep. No more keeping our relationship a secret."

"I can't—"

"I mean it. I'm done sneaking around."

"I mean, I can't do it today. I'm having Sunday dinner with my parents." She frowned, considering. "We eat around two. Maybe we can meet up later?"

He hesitated only a moment. "Can I come?"

"You can't seriously want to have dinner with my parents."

"Why not?"

"'Cause they're my parents. Why would you possibly want to meet a middle-aged, Mexican couple?"

"Because they're your parents," he said slowly. "Unless they don't want to meet me, I want to meet them."

"I—" she began, but then broke off. "Okay. You can meet my parents. But don't say I didn't warn you."

He left quickly after that, but as he made his way back to his condo, he wasn't able to shake the uneasy feeling he had about Ana losing her virginity. As calm and blasé as she seemed, he still wished he'd known ahead of time. Then he could have... what?

All the same questions she'd badgered him with flitted through his mind. In the end, he reached the same conclusion she had.

He wouldn't have done anything differently. Except, maybe she was right. Maybe he would have choked. But maybe not. In the end, the only conclusion he could come to was that he simply wanted it to matter to her. Because it mattered to him.

So much for her plan to quietly lose her virginity without him even noticing. That plan had gone about as well as her plan to quietly introduce him to her family.

"We could go see a movie instead," she offered Ward. It was her fifth attempt to distract him since he'd shown up on her doorstep ten minutes earlier.

"No." He grimaced as he helped her into the passenger side of his Lexus. "You're jaded about Hollywood, remember? I don't think moviegoing would be particularly relaxing. Besides, they're expecting you."

"They'd get over it." She'd never hear the end of it if she canceled now. But she was still trying to talk him out of it. "It's not like I have dinner with them every Sunday." Of course, she did, actually eat with them every Sunday, but that just sounded lame.

Ward shook his head anyway. "I'm looking forward to meeting your parents."

"Great." She smothered a groan. A moment later, as he started the car, she directed him to head west on Claremont.

He flicked on his blinker, but sent her a puzzled look. "I

thought your parents still lived on the Worths' estate, over by the coast."

"They do." She had to unclench her jaw to explain. "We're not having dinner there." She paused, hoping he'd let it go, but he didn't. Finally, she explained, "When my parents found out I was bringing a date, they decided a mere meal in their apartment wasn't enough. So we're going to my uncle Julio's house."

Ward flashed her a charming smile. "Oh, are they fans?"

"Of you? No, they've probably never heard of you. But I've never brought a date anywhere. The mere idea of me in the company of a man was enough to excite their anticipation."

He must have picked up on the dread in her voice. "What exactly can I expect?"

She blew out a harsh breath, decided honesty was the best policy and delivered the blow. "A full-blown party. Thirty, maybe forty people."

He gave a bark of laughter that sounded incredulous. Maybe even a little nervous. If he was wise, it would be nerves.

"I thought you said you were from a small family."

"Small immediate family," she corrected. "Just me and my parents. But I have ten aunts and uncles here in the States, all within driving distance. I have nearly thirty cousins. Plus spouses."

He blew out an impressed whistle. "And kids?"

"So many you'll be nervous you're going to step on one when you're crossing the room." For the first time since they got in the car she dared to look at him. He looked neither shocked nor horrified. Which she took as a good sign. "We can still call and cancel," she offered.

"No." He flashed her a cocky smile. "I'm looking forward to it."

She gave him a few directions as he steered the car toward her uncle's neighborhood. It was much like hers, but a little older, a little shabbier, a little more working-class. The houses were small, but built early enough in the California property boom that the yards were spacious and well shaded with fruit trees.

It wouldn't compare to his condo on the beach—let alone the

house in Harleston Village, but somehow she had the feeling he wouldn't mind. Ward was remarkably unfussy and unpretentious. Wealth didn't seem to impress him much. And she knew from the dive he'd taken her to in Charleston that he valued good food over ambiance. And if there was one thing her big, extended family did well, it was good food.

He turned the Lexus onto her uncle's street and she offered once more, "Last chance to ditch?"

His grin broadened. "No way. Anything that has you this nervous, I've got to see."

Her grumble of indignation was cut short, because a moment later he pulled the car to the curb—nearly half a block away because of the cars lining the street. Even from the safety of Ward's car, she could feel the energy and excitement buzzing around her uncle's house. Some of the kids had started a game of soccer on the front lawn. A couple of the older teenagers were slouching grumpily on the front steps, all defiant bravado. Music could be heard blaring from the backyard. Someone had already fired up the grill and the air was laden with the pungent sent of charred oak.

On any other day, the sights, sounds and smells of a family cookout would fill her heart with pure joy. Today it only rattled her nerves. She didn't expect Ward to turn up his nose at her relatives. He just wasn't that kind of guy. She was less confident about all of her relatives being completely welcoming to him. She didn't get along with everyone in her extended family and there was a chance some people would see toting a celebrity along to a family dinner as a way of showing off. But even deeper was her fear that this afternoon was going to shift their relationship in some subtle way. And that the change might be even more important than the one that had taken place last night.

Then, she'd merely taken him into her bed. Now, she was truly letting him into her life.

Ana didn't seem to relax much once they reached the party. And Ward was too cued into her moods to enjoy himself if she wasn't having a good time. Enjoy himself much, anyway.

Nilda, Ana's mother, greeted him with barely repressed joy. If Ana hadn't warned him that she'd never brought a guy home, he might have been surprised by Nilda's speculative gaze and exuberant hug. Nilda squeezed him so affectionately, he nearly couldn't breathe.

"I warned you," Ana muttered under her breath once he was released.

Juan, Ana's father, was more naturally reserved. A balding, gray-haired man, he carried himself with a sort of old-world dignity that belied his diminutive height and expansive girth. He shook Ward's hand firmly in a way that told Ward he was being sized up.

Somehow he doubted that either his profession or his wealth were in his favor. "My Ana," Juan said seriously in heavily accented English. He stood close enough to Ward not to be overheard. "She is like a rose, delicate, beautiful…" He waggled his hand in an iffy gesture. "But the stem of the rose is tough. You can't easily separate it from its bush. If you are not careful, either you will get scratched, or you will crush the blossom and then it will wither and die—" he snapped his fingers "—very quickly. You understand?"

Ward nodded. "I do, sir."

Juan gave him one last assessing look and then slapped him heartily on the arm. "Very good. Come and have a *cerveza*."

After that, Ward didn't talk to Ana for another hour or two. Her father guided him around, introducing him to friends and relatives. Most of the men had congregated in the backyard, whereas the women had holed up in the kitchen. This far inland, the temperature was warmer. The weather was unexpectedly warm for February and the ice-cold beer was all the more refreshing when sipped under the expansive shade of an avocado tree. There were kids playing on the lawn, and plenty of parents around to shoo them away from the barbecue pit where carne asada and *cabrito* were being grilled. Women streamed constantly in and out of the house carrying trays of food. Someone had set a radio out on the patio and a steady stream of Ozomatli tunes had been playing. With their unique combination of Latino hip-hop and urban world beat, Ozomatli was one of his favorite Los Angeles bands. All in all, he couldn't have picked a more festive setting.

Comparing this to the elegant party of the previous evening, he had a new appreciation for why Ana hadn't wanted to go the Hudsons' party. This was much more fun.

What worried him was that she didn't seem to be enjoying it. Sure, she spent plenty of time talking to her relatives, but he could clearly read her posture. Stiff and unyielding. Awkward. Like she didn't fit in and was waiting for someone else to notice. It was telling that she'd actually seemed more comfortable at the party the previous evening. Here she just seemed ill at ease.

There was only one person who seemed even less comfortable among the boisterous crowd: Ricky. Ward was surprised, but not shocked, when he spotted Ricky slouching among some of the older kids. He went over to say hello, exchanged a few words and even met Ricky's mother. He'd seen Ricky once since he'd returned from Charleston. He could tell already that Ricky would be a tough nut to crack. But the kid liked music. And he wasn't any tougher than Ward had been at that age.

As soon as Ricky's mother, Lena, went off to check on something inside, Ricky leveled a serious stare at Ward.

Chest puffed out, full of protective belligerence, he said, "So you're dating my cousin?"

"I suppose I am."

"We don't see Ana much, but we take care of our own. Don't mess with her."

For a second, Ward could only stare at Ricky in surprise. Ricky was all of about five feet four inches. And maybe just barely a hundred pounds. Yet here he was, ready to defend Ana's honor.

Ward quirked an eyebrow and tried to keep his tone serious. "You're warning me off?"

Ricky bumped his chin up, like he suspected Ward was making fun of him. "We take care of our own," he repeated.

Yeah, Ward recognized that stubborn expression. It was more than mere family resemblance.

Nodding his understanding, Ward said, "She's lucky to have you. I hope she knows just how lucky. I hope you do, too."

He didn't have any trouble with the sincerity of those words. No wonder Ricky was such a great kid—his inclination toward truancy aside. Whatever Ana's family lacked in financial resources or social standing, they more than made up for with their open affection. He'd never been a part of a large family. After only a few hours in their company, he could feel himself getting drawn in by the comfort of their companionship.

He could easily imagine quickly becoming as attached to them as he now was to Ana herself.

Just then, he noticed Ana up on her toes, peering over the heads of others to catch his eye. She looked at him with raised eyebrows, the question written clearly on her face: Was he okay? Did he need rescuing?

He smiled and waved her away. She frowned and shuffled off. Instantly, he was sorry that he hadn't called her over. He missed having her by his side. Just missed her.

And in that instant, he knew how completely he'd been fooling himself about his ability to maintain his emotional distance from her. He should have known that evening he'd caught her watching the television special on him. She'd pegged his crap so effectively. In that moment, she'd seen him more clearly than he'd ever seen himself. It had taken this long for him to even admit that she was right.

Hell, if that hadn't clued him in to the fact that he was in serious trouble, last night at her house should have done the job. After they'd had sex, she'd calmly gotten up to get dressed and he'd damn near been in tears. If that wasn't a sign of how deeply in over his head he was, he didn't know what was. Add to that the fact that he was just about ready to start exchanging Christmas cards with her family, and he was completely screwed.

No. Forget that. He was just in love.

And it just sucked. Because she was so obviously not in love with him. Even if she thought she was now, she sure wouldn't be for long. She'd pegged him on the crap about the Alvarez. She'd see through the rest of it soon enough.

If he was a stronger man, he might wait around for her to walk away on her own. But he didn't think he'd survive her leaving him. Which meant it was time to quietly extract himself from her life.

Twelve

Once people started serving food, Ana gave up all pretense of maintaining a conversation with her aunt and went searching for Ward. She found him sitting on the cement block border that edged a flower bed. He sat with a plate carefully balanced on one knee, the dark waves of his hair shining in the dappled sun that filtered through the lemon tree. She sat down beside him with her own plate loaded with *cabrito* and charro beans.

She finished chewing her bite, then asked, "Has it been awful?"

"Not so bad." He took another sip of his Dos Equis. "Humbling."

"How so?" she asked, raising a glass of iced tea to sip.

"None of them know my music," he explained with mock indignation. "Not one of them."

She laughed, holding her hand to her mouth to keep from spewing her drink. Swallowing, she added, "Oh, you poor little famous boy."

"Actually, it's kind of nice. First time in decades I've gone to a party where no one knew who I was."

"Oh, the women all know. Trust me. It's been like a Senate hearing in there." She stabbed her guacamole with a chip. "However, it is better than the last family get-together when I had to field thinly veiled questions about my sexuality from Aunt Celica, who just started watching *Ellen* and was convinced I was a lesbian." She expected him to laugh at that. When he didn't, she searched his face and found his expression oddly distant. "They've been okay, though? No one's too pushy?"

"Not at all. I was surprised to see Ricky here."

Now the boy stood in front of the food-laden picnic table. He was dressed much as he had been every other time she'd seen him. Like ninety-five percent of all American teenage boys, Ricky's pants were too baggy and barely held on his hips by a belt. He wore a white tank top under an unbuttoned long-sleeve shirt. If he wasn't in a gang already, he was trying very hard to look like he was.

Ana followed Ward's gaze and frowned. "You know Ricky?"

"He's the kid I've been mentoring."

"My Ricky is *that* Ricky?"

He chewed for a minute and then explained, "I didn't know you were related until just now."

Ana stared at him, obviously surprised. "I had no idea Ricky had been to Hannah's Hope." She shook her head. "I can't believe I didn't figure that out. You must think I'm a horrible aunt."

"I think you've been pretty busy." He nodded in Lena's direction. "If she's your cousin, why wouldn't she come in herself? Why did her son have to manipulate her into coming?"

Ana's gaze wandered over to where Lena stood by the back door. Despite the fact that she was only a few years older than Ana, age and weariness already lined her face.

"Lena and I aren't exactly what you'd call close."

"Why not?" he asked.

"You know all those stereotypes I told you my parents wanted me to avoid? Lena followed every damn one of them. Her father is my dad's older brother. Her parents helped bring my parents over. Lena's three years older than me. We lived two blocks away when we lived in L.A. She got pregnant at fifteen. That's when my parents moved us to Vista del Mar. She never finished high school. She works hard, but barely scrapes by." Not for the first time, she tried to imagine herself in Lena's shoes. Tried and failed miserably. "And now, she's worried about Ricky staying in school."

"I thought you said you weren't close?"

Ana smiled wryly. "We aren't. That hasn't kept the family grapevine quiet."

"Do you think that's why she didn't come into Hannah's Hope herself?" he prodded.

Ana shot him a surprised look. "I don't know. Maybe. She doesn't like me." She blew out a frustrated breath. "But she also has a butt-load of pride. That could be it, too." And then she laughed, looking around the yard. "She's not the only one. Half the people here work for Worth Industries in one way or the other. They're all scared about the future. No one knows what it means that so many of the uppity-ups from Worth Industries are leaving. But none of them want to admit that they need help."

Abruptly, she set her plate aside, leaving much of her food untouched, and turned to face him more fully. "This is why what we're doing at Hannah's Hope is so important. You see that, don't you?"

"I saw that before," he countered, annoyance creeping into his voice. "I just wonder if you see it."

"What's that supposed to mean?"

"I'm talking about your job at Hannah's Hope." His tone was serious. Harsher than his normal gravelly charm. "You're burying yourself under paperwork because you're afraid of getting out in the community and actually dealing with people."

"That is ridiculous," she protested. Standing abruptly, she crossed to the trash can by the back door and dumped her plate in.

He followed a few steps behind, dumped his own plate and then followed her in to the now deserted kitchen. Everyone else was out in the back, enjoying the food, which left them alone in the tiny, homey kitchen.

"So ridiculous that you storm off in response?" he prodded.

She stopped and spun to face him, then poked a finger in the direction of his chest. "Don't you dare tell me I'm not doing my job."

"The administrative crap is only half of running Hannah's Hope. That's the easy part. The hard part is getting volunteers to commit their time and energy to making it work. And the really hard part is reaching out to people and getting them to accept help."

His words stung and she turned away from him, busying herself collecting the many bowls and utensils that had been left scattered over the counter once the food was prepared. "You think I don't know how hard that's going to be?" She dropped the biggest of the bowls in the sink basin and turned on the water to fill it. "You think I don't know a thing or two about the stubborn pride that goes along with poverty and lack of education?" She grabbed the bottle of dish soap and gave it a vicious squirt. "Because I do. I know all about that. I grew up among these people. I know precisely how hard it's going to be to get them to accept help."

"Is that why you haven't been talking up Hannah's Hope to the people here today?"

"I—" Her mouth gaped open as she struggled to find a fitting response. Finally, she snapped her mouth closed, then said through clenched teeth, "You're right." She grabbed a deadly looking butcher knife and dropped it into the bowl of sudsy water. "I haven't been talking about Hannah's Hope. But this is my family. And it's difficult and—"

"And that's why you haven't gone over to talk to Lena? Even though you know she's a perfect candidate for Hannah's Hope? Because it's difficult?"

She added more dishes—a few more bowls and some spatulas—to the growing tower of dirty dishes. "That's not fair."

"But somehow it is fair that you're ignoring her needs because they make you uncomfortable?"

Even though she didn't so much as glance in his direction, she was painfully aware of the intensity of his gaze.

"But maybe you think she really isn't a good candidate," he

added, his tone glib as he turned away from her to prop his hips against the counter perpendicular to the sink.

Ana snatched up a cutting board and wedged it behind the tower of bowls, but she didn't leap to Lena's defense.

"Maybe you think she's screwed up everything in her life so far," he continued. "How could she possibly handle all the extra work it would take to actually commit to getting her GED?"

She slammed down the final bowl. The tower of dirty dishes crashed into the sink, splattering water, bubbles and bits of food across the counter and her shirt. "Don't you judge her! You have no idea what it's like being a poor Latina woman in this country."

Ward gave a humorless laugh, finally turning to face her again. "Yeah, well, I suspect you have no idea what that's like, either."

She gasped, shock at his words making her light-headed. "I can't believe you just said that."

Instantly, his gaze softened. "It's what you believe, isn't it? That you're different. That you can't relate to their struggles." For a long moment he just looked at her as if taking in every emotion flickering across her face. As if he saw everything she desperately wanted to hide, but somehow couldn't. Finally, he shook his head. His eyes were sad, his tone gentle. "I don't believe it," he said slowly. "But it's pretty obvious to me that you do. Otherwise, you would have laughed it off. Or more likely, you would have socked me in the jaw."

She pressed her lips in a compact line, blinking back tears that she refused to let him see. "So what was that? Some kind of test?"

"No. I was making a point."

"Why would you say that to me? What kind of point would be so important you'd have to—"

But she broke off. If she wasn't going to cry in front of him, then she damn well wasn't going to tell him point-blank that he'd just skewered her emotionally.

Just when she least expected his tenderness—when she least

wanted it—he gently cupped her chin and tilted it up, forcing her to meet his gaze.

"I said those things because I had to." His tone was gentle. As sincere as she'd ever heard it. "You have it in you to be an incredible nonprofit director. But you have to get over your fear that the community will reject you if you reach out to them. You can do amazing things for Hannah's Hope, but I won't always be here to push you."

His words sucked the air right out of her lungs. Actually, suffocating couldn't have hurt more.

There it was. He'd all but announced his intention of leaving her. Now that they'd had sex, he was no longer interested in her. He was being as polite as he could about it, but it still hurt.

She'd known their relationship wouldn't last forever. Known she'd never live up to Cara's memory. But she'd never dreamed him leaving her would feel like this.

She pulled her gaze away from his. Focused her eyes on an obscenely cheerful blue-and-yellow tile behind him.

"Well, then," she said. "I guess you have me all figured out. It's good to know that your duties as a board member extend to psychoanalyzing the employees."

"I didn't say that as a board member."

"Yeah, I knew that." She forced herself to look him in the eye again. She wanted him to know that she'd gotten the message. He hadn't said it as a board member, but as her boyfriend.

Or rather, not her boyfriend. But the guy she'd slept with the previous night. What was it he'd said a moment ago? He wanted to say this now because he wasn't always going to be around to push her. Yeah. She got that. Good thing she hadn't expected him to be around forever.

She just hadn't expected the breakup to hurt this badly.

It was obvious from Ana's expression that she didn't want him touching her at all. Probably ever again.

"Okay, then," she announced roughly. "As long as we're putting it all out on the table and being completely honest, as long as we're talking about what would be best for Hannah's

Hope, I don't really think you're stepping up and doing your part, either."

He had not seen that coming. He'd heard the pain in her voice, but he still hadn't expected her to lash out. "How's that?"

"What about Rafe?" she asked sternly.

Her words were so unexpected, it took a second for them to register. "What about Rafe?"

She gave a shrug that was part false confidence, and part pure, ballsy anger. "You're his friend. You can talk to him. Influence him."

"Whatever influence you think I have over him," he said slowly, "it doesn't extend to business decisions. If he's thinking of closing the factory, there's not much I can do about that."

"I'm not talking about the factory." The water she'd been running in the sink had nearly reached the edge and she reached over to turn it off with a jerk of the handle. "I'm talking about his involvement with Hannah's Hope. Or rather his complete lack of involvement."

He stepped away from her, once again propping his hips against the counter. He kept his tone carefully blank. "What exactly do you expect me to do?"

She picked up one of those long-handled scrubbers that people used to wash their dishes. But instead of using it, she gestured with it. "For starters you can talk him into coming to the street fair on Saturday. No matter how many times I've called him, I can't get him to commit to being there. But the people of this town need reassurances that only he can give them. They need to know that even if he dismantles Worth Industries and sells it off bit by bit, he's still committed to Hannah's Hope."

"And you think him showing up at the festival will do that? You think it will magically convince everyone he's a great guy?"

"I'm not suggesting he come to make balloon animals and eat cotton candy. He should say a few words."

"About what?"

"Hannah's Hope is in honor of his mother. Surely that means something to him."

"In other words, you want him to trot out his grief and parade it around to reassure the citizens of Vista del Mar."

"That's not what I said." She poked the scrubber in his direction, wielding it like a sword. "You're being obtuse."

"Excuse me if I don't think Rafe talking about his mother is going to make anyone feel any better at all."

"How can you not have sympathy for these people? They need someone to stand up for them. They need an advocate. They feel helpless in the face of Rafe's power. And if you could just imagine what that feels like—"

Tired of waiting to be swatted with that damn scrubber, he snatched it out of her hand and tossed it on the counter, out of her reach. "Don't think for a minute that I don't know what it feels like to be helpless and scared. I know all about that." His tone was harsh. His voice foreign to his own ears. "If you think the threat of losing your job is scary, well, I gotta tell you, it's nothing compared to the fear of losing your wife. So I know all too well what fear is like and the kinds of things it does to you."

Ana looked up at him, her eyes wide and filled with anguish. For a second, he thought she might even cry. Or maybe apologize. He didn't think he'd be able to stomach either of those reactions.

But instead, she wrapped her arms around her waist as if she were unbearably cold. When she spoke, her tone was brittle and bruised. "It always comes back to her, doesn't it?"

"I don't know what you mean." The anger that had been so close to the surface just a second ago faded.

She continued talking, almost as if she hadn't heard him. "Everything always comes back to her. Cara's right there under the surface. No matter what else is going on in your life. You won't push Rafe to trot out his grief in public, because you've never gotten over having grieved for her that way." Ana sucked in a deep breath, like she need strength to continue. "You're right. I don't know what it's like to lose a spouse to cancer. I hope I never know what that's like. But I can't be in a relationship with someone whose entire existence is centered around that one experience."

"That's not true," he said, trying to deny it.

"Then why haven't you sold the house? Why haven't you gotten rid of her sunglasses? Or her art collections? Why don't you play the Alvarez?" She met his gaze, her own eyes wide and tearful. "I can't do this anymore. I think you should leave."

What could he say to that? He could hardly beg her to reconsider. Not when he knew she was making the right decision for herself. All he could do was nod and say, "Fair enough."

"Ward, I'm—"

He abruptly let her go and turned away.

"—sorry."

And with that, he stormed out, before his anger really got the better of him. He didn't take any comfort in knowing that he'd done right by Hannah's Hope. In knowing that even if he'd hurt her, he'd done right by her, too. He'd seen the flash of pain in her eyes. Heard the anguish in her voice.

He'd pushed her away. Maybe that's what he'd been trying to do all along. Either way, he was pretty sure he'd just done a bang up job of crushing the rose.

The day after the barbecue at Ana's uncle's home, Ward found Ricky's house about three blocks away. The tiny bungalow where Ricky lived with his mother sat on a scorched swath of dead grass with a rusting bike in the front yard and an even rustier late-model compact car at the curb.

Though Ward had been up since his dawn run on the beach, he waited until after ten to drop by Ricky's house. There were some things even stardom couldn't excuse and Ward knew from experience that waking up a night owl too early was one of them.

Ricky answered the door after the first knock, dressed in his standard baggy jeans and sweatshirt. He appeared to have just woken up, despite the fact that it was a school day. Ricky made a shushing gesture as he nodded toward what was obviously a back bedroom, then led him back to the kitchen where a box of cereal sat open beside an empty bowl.

Ricky slid the kitchen door closed and said, "*Mi mamá* is still sleeping. She got a job on the cleaning crew at the plant."

"That's great."

Ricky gave a defeated shrug. "As long as the plant stays open."

Ward didn't want to say how unlikely he feared that would be. Instead, he asked, "Why aren't you in school? I thought you said you wouldn't skip anymore."

"It's a teacher work day." Ricky held up his hands in a gesture of innocence. "I swear!" He poured some cereal into his bowl and shoveled a spoonful into his mouth. As an afterthought, he raised the box up in silent offer.

"No, thanks." The sugar-coated, neon puffs barely resembled food.

"Why're you slumming?" Ricky asked through a mouthful.

"I…" Now that it was time to explain, Ward choked. With a sigh, he turned around one of the kitchen chairs and sat on it with his arms braced over the back. "Next week, after the street fair, I'm leaving Vista del Mar for a while. I wanted to tell you myself."

Ricky's gaze dropped to his bowl. He shoveled in another spoonful of neon puffs, his face as expressionless as a placid cow as he chewed. Then he ate another bite before shrugging. "Okay."

The boy's studied lack of response said more about his emotional state than he probably knew.

"Ricky, I need you to know that this has nothing to do with you. I'll make sure Ana finds you a great mentor to replace me. I'm sorry we only met a couple of times."

"Naw, man." He waved a negligent hand. "It's okay. No big deal, right?"

"I wish I could stay, but I just can't."

"No, I get it." In went another bite of food. "Who wants to hang around here and mentor some stupid kid, right? I mean, you probably have, like, concerts to plan and stuff."

"It's not that. You're a great kid." Ward reached out a hand and laid it on Ricky's arm. "You're smart and—"

"Stop it." Ricky shook off Ward's hand with annoyance.

"I mean it. I've enjoyed knowing you. You're—"

"You don't have to kiss my ass, okay? You can go back to your real life without feeling guilty."

"I wasn't trying to do that," Ward explained, trying to keep his own frustration from his voice. "I was being honest."

"Well, you sound like a sleazebag."

Great. And now he was being criticized by a teenager. Just barely a teenager. "I was going for honest, but if that's sleazy to you, so be it. You want the truth? We broke up. Ana dumped me. So I decided to leave. To make it easier on her. I'm—"

Ricky burst out laughing. "She dumped you?"

"Yes. She dumped me." Ward waited for Ricky's peals of laughter to die down. "But I'm glad you find my broken heart funny."

Ricky just shook his head, clearly still amused, even though he was no longer laughing. "I just didn't think you were the kind of guy to get dumped. I mean, dude, you're rich."

"Yeah, well, rich guys get dumped, too."

"Did you really dig her?" Ricky asked quietly.

"Yeah, I did," Ward said after a thoughtful moment. What would have been the point in lying?

"I saw you two at the party. She was into you. So why are you leaving?"

"She saw through all the smoke and mirrors." Ricky just looked at him blankly. "You know, smoke and mirrors. From *The Wizard of Oz?* No?"

Ricky ignored the reference and asked, "You're not even going to fight for her. What's up with that?"

"She was pretty clear. She doesn't want me." And then, for reasons he didn't quite understand, he found himself opening up to Ricky. "I can't make her fall in love with me."

Ricky smirked. "Can't you just tell her how you feel? Write her a song or something."

Ward sighed. If only it was that easy. 'Cause, sure. He could write her a song. He could pull out all the stops and charm the pants off her. But then he'd never really know if he'd won her back or if she'd just fallen in love with the musician.

That wasn't something a kid like Ricky could understand.

Before he could attempt to explain it, Ricky finished chewing his bite and added, "Just make it a good one. Not a cheesy one like your others."

"First I sound like a sleazebag, and now my songs are cheesy?" Why was he even talking to this kid? "Wait a second. I thought you hadn't heard any of my music."

Ricky shrugged. "I downloaded some of your songs."

"You didn't even pay for them? You're insulting my music and you didn't even—"

"Hey, I paid for them. My grandparents gave me an iTunes gift card for Christmas. I'm poor. I'm not a thief."

Mollified—just slightly—Ward pressed, "But you thought they were cheesy."

"I guess you play guitar pretty good."

"Yeah," he said drily. "I guess."

It was a good thing he had those multiple walls full of platinum albums to fall back on, because this kid was kicking his ego's butt.

"I just thought your lyrics were… I don't know. Sappy." Ricky studied him with his head tilted to the side. "Do chicks usually dig that?"

"Yes. They usually do."

"Maybe you've been dating the wrong kind of girl."

Ward blew out a long breath. The kid had sure said a mouthful there. "This is crazy. I'm not going to take romantic advice from a kid."

"Whatever." Ricky gave another little shrug. "But I've known her longer."

"Okay, then. What's your point?"

Ricky leaned forward, gesturing sharply. "A woman like Ana, she's tough, man. She's not gonna fall for some guy just 'cause he's smooth. She's too smart for that."

"Okay, mister fourteen-year-old-expert-on-women, what do you suggest?"

Ricky held up his palms in a sign of innocence. "Hey, I've lived with a single mother my whole life. Do you have any idea how many times I've seen *The Notebook?*"

That was actually a good point. Ward lowered himself into the chair opposite Ricky. "So what do you suggest?" he asked seriously. And then mentally kicked himself. Because if he was legitimately going to follow the advice of a fourteen-year-old boy, the situation was truly desperate. And then he realized, desperate or not, he loved Ana and she was worth fighting for.

"All I know is that at the end of the movie, Rachel McAdams doesn't end up with the rich, charming guy. She ends up with the guy who really loves her."

Well, that was the kicker, wasn't it? Ward sat back in his chair.

"I do really love her," Ward mused aloud. "But she sees through all my tricks."

Ricky gave him a *well-duh* look. "You don't use a trick."

The most obvious solution, but also the most painful. And still a long shot.

Thirteen

Part of her expected Ward to show up again on her doorstep. Or at least come into the office. But when one hour passed and then another, she realized she had to accept a grim reality. She'd asked him to leave and he'd taken her at her word.

It didn't matter that she knew she'd made the smart choice. It didn't matter that she knew their relationship had come to its logical end. Her heart still ached for what might have been.

No. Not even that. Her heart ached for what she imagined might be possible.

The honest truth was, she'd known going into it that they had no future. She'd known he still loved Cara. She'd simply let herself ignore the obvious. For a little while.

Of course she couldn't bring herself to regret anything she'd done. She'd gained too much by knowing him. Obviously, there was the mind-blowing passion to consider. But even more, there was the insight into herself.

She felt as though she'd barely known herself until now.

Ward, for all his flaws—if loving his wife could truly be

a flaw—had seen her more truly than she'd ever seen herself. He'd pointed out the lies she'd told herself to hide her deepest fears. And if she loved him at all, then the least she could do was respect the memory of their relationship enough to honor that.

Which was how she ended up parked on the street outside of Lena's house just before noon. Just in time to see Ward leaving. She'd recognized his Lexus parked on the curb and so had parked her own sedan a few doors down, crouched low in her seat and waited.

Biting down on her lower lip and cupping her hand beside her sunglasses, she watched as Ward shook hands with Ricky. He gave the boy an *attaboy* slap to the arm. Then Ward walked out to his car, climbed in and drove away without even glancing in her direction. Which she supposed was to be expected. It was a miracle he'd ever glanced in her direction to begin with.

She waited five minutes to make sure he wasn't going to turn around and come back, having forgotten his sunglasses or something. And then she waited another five for the knot in her throat to loosen. Then she climbed out of her car and walked up to Lena's door, cursing the way fate had put her and Ward in the same place at the same time. It was bad enough that she'd still have to work with him occasionally for Hannah's Hope. Why did she have to see him today, when she was already feeling so emotionally vulnerable?

When she knocked on the door, Ricky answered right away. His gaze widened in surprise and he gave a nervous little glance down the block as if to verify that Ward was truly gone.

"Ana. ¿Cómo estás?"

"I'm good. Is your mom here?"

"Ward just left," Ricky said, instead of answering. His posture was belligerent. Protective almost.

"I saw that," she answered.

Apparently, Ricky was hoping she'd press him for more information, because his expression soured into a snarl. "Don't you want to know why he was here?"

She really didn't. The less time Ward spent in her brain, the faster she'd recover. But Ricky obviously had no interest in protecting her. "Fine. Why was he here?"

"He was saying goodbye. He's going back to Charleston."

That defensive challenge was so strong in Ricky's gaze, she couldn't say anything.

"Look, I'm sorry. I know you really liked him."

"He's leaving because you broke his heart," Ricky accused.

"He told you that?"

"He didn't have to. I'm not an idiot."

"Right." And now she felt like that bad guy. What a fantastic day this was turning into. "Is your mom here or not?"

As if on cue, the door to one of the bedrooms opened and Lena propped her shoulder against the doorjamb. She was dressed in a robe, her hair mussed from sleep, her scowl already in place.

"What do you want?" she asked, her unspoken message—you don't belong here—just as clear as her spoken one.

"I just wanted to talk," Ana offered. She gave Ricky a pointed look and he was smart enough to excuse himself.

"I'll be in my room, *Mamá*," he said. As if she might need him to protect her from the big, bad Ana, when the reverse was probably far closer to the truth.

Once Ricky left, Lena's scowl deepened. "You don't have to look at me like that. I got a job working on the cleaning crew at the factory. That's why I'm just getting up. Not 'cause I was out all night partying."

Ana held up her palms. "I didn't say anything."

"You were thinking it," Lena accused.

"Honestly, Lena—" Then Ana forced out a sigh. No need to make things worse. "Look, I know you don't like me. I know you think I'm spoiled."

"And?" Lena asked with an arched brow.

Well. There she had it. It sure would have been nice if Lena had denied it. But since she hadn't… "But I need a favor."

"Why would I do you a favor?"

"Because the favor is I want you to accept a job at Hannah's Hope."

Lena's gaze turned even more suspicious. If that was possible.

Ana could see the sneering anger ready to burst forth, so she jumped in before Lena's indignation could overwhelm her pride.

"Just hear me out." Lena studied her for a second before giving a little nod. "It's come to my attention that I'm not reaching out to the community the way I need to." She sighed, finding this harder than she expected. "Ward pointed it out actually. He thinks I'm afraid of being rejected. I don't know. Maybe he's right. I don't know what it's like to be poor. I know what it's like to be unlucky, but I don't know what it's like to be down on my luck. But you do."

Lena sneered. "So what? You want me to teach you what it's like to be poor? Isn't that backward?"

"No. I don't need anyone to teach me. I just need someone who's been there. Someone people will trust."

Lena's lower lip jutted out. "I'm not the kind of person people trust."

"Well, you will be."

For just a second, the suspicion faded from Lena's gaze to reveal a flicker of hope. Seeing her chance, Ana started talking fast. "I can't pay you much, but I can beat the cleaning crew at the plant. And the hours will be better. But you'll have to work on your getting your GED in your off-hours. We'll need to get you fully qualified within a year, I'd think."

"What makes you so sure I'd want to work for you?"

"Because you believe in Hannah's Hope. I know you do or you wouldn't let Ricky go there. And I honestly don't know if we can be successful without you."

Ana could see Lena wavering. And she knew she'd win her over. She had to. She didn't think she could take any more disappointment.

Before Ana could think of anything else with which to entice

Lena, Ricky stuck his head through the door and yelled, "Come on, *Mamá,* just take the job!"

Lena's expression softened. Then she smiled. "Well. I guess that settles it."

Three days before the street fair, and her personal life in apparent shambles, Ana could think of about ten thousand things she'd rather do besides talk to a reporter. But when Gillian Mitchell from the *Seaside Gazette* called, Ana had little choice but to take her call. After all, Christi—who had dated the editor years ago—had called the guy several times hoping the *Gazette* would run a story about the street fair on the front page that Saturday.

The street fair seemed a pretty fluffy piece compared to the kinds of things Gillian covered, but if they wanted to put their ace reporter on it, who was Ana to complain?

However, she was not prepared for Gillian's questions.

"Rumor has it that Ward Miller is planning on performing at the open house. This would be his first public performance in over three years. And the first single on the new album he's been working on."

For a second, Ana nearly laughed. As her surprise subsided, she weighed her options. Disappoint the reporter too much and she might not get the good placement they needed. But she didn't want to toy with her, either. Finally, she hedged, "Ward is involved in a lot of charities. I'm sure they'd all love to claim his first public performance in three years."

On the other end of the line, Gillian hesitated. Finally, in a tone that hinted at frustration, she said, "He may be involved in a lot of charities, but he hasn't been involved with a lot of charity directors. I'd say his personal attachment to you changes things."

Ana rocked back in her chair. "Oh."

"I've surprised you." Again, Gillian's tone shifted. "I'm sorry I was so blunt. I thought you were blowing me off."

"I wasn't," Ana said honestly. "Despite what you may have

heard about my relationship with Ward—there's no way he's playing a song—new or otherwise—at the street fair."

Gillian didn't respond right away, so Ana continued.

"I'm sorry. I'm sure that's not the big story you were hoping for. But Ward's involvement with Hannah's Hope is strictly as a board member and supporter. He'll be attending the street fair in that capacity."

At least she hoped he would. Since she hadn't spoken to him since Sunday evening, for all she knew, he'd changed his plans and was on his way back to Charleston already.

"You sound really sure," Gillian said, confusion in her voice.

Ana thought of Cara's sunglasses sitting on the console by the door. Thought of the empty house he didn't live in and the tiny carriage house to which he'd exiled himself. She thought of the Alvarez sitting in a glass display case at CMF, forever, eternally unplayed.

And then, thinking of the big fight they'd had, she figured the chances of him even showing up at the street festival were pretty slim. Forget playing at it.

"Yes. I'm very sure." Then she thought of the annoyance in Gillian's tone just a moment ago when the other woman had thought Ana was lying to her. "Wait a second. You sound pretty sure yourself."

"I… You know," Gillian said with sudden cheer. "I must have been mistaken. Thanks for your help."

A second later, the line went dead.

Ana pulled the handset away from her head and stared at it suspiciously. She replaced the handset in the cradle, turned back to her computer and drummed her fingers mindlessly on her keyboard. Then looked up the number for the *Gazette* on Google, called it and a moment later had the front desk connect her to Gillian's phone.

"You sounded really sure," Ana repeated.

"I didn't," Gillian protested.

"No. You did. You were actually annoyed when you thought I was putting you off. What's up?"

"There's nothing up!" But Gillian's voice sounded high and strained. She may be used to asking tough questions, but she wasn't used to being in the hot seat herself.

"Who did you talk to that made you think he'd be performing at the open house?" Because God help her, if Christi had out-and-out lied to the editor to get him to run the story...

"A reporter never gives up her sources," Gillian said sternly.

"Right," Ana quipped. "This isn't exactly high political intrigue we're talking about. It's entertainment gossip. Who is this source of yours?"

"Look, I just…" Gillian stammered. Then she released a sigh. "If he's planning some big romantic gesture, I don't want to be the one to ruin it."

"If who is planning some big romantic gesture?"

"Ward."

Ana's heart stuttered in her chest. Ward? Planning a big romantic gesture? For her?

A bark of bitter laughter bubbled out. Gillian seemed not to notice it.

"My big source," Gillian continued, "is his assistant. He called to schedule an interview with me for immediately after the street fair. He's the one who told me about the song and new album."

Ana's heart started thudding dully again in her chest. "You mean Ryan. His new public relations manager."

"No, that wasn't his name." On the other end of the phone, Ana heard Gillian clicking away on her computer as if pulling up a file. "Jess was his name. And he said he was Ward's assistant."

Ana frowned, rocking slowly back and forth in her chair. Ryan, she totally would have expected this of him. He wouldn't have any trouble misleading a reporter to get better press coverage. But it wasn't like Jess at all. "And it was Jess who told you about the performance?" Ana asked, still trying to wrap her mind around it.

"Yes. He said Ward was going to perform. That it was the first new song he'd written in years and that it was off the new album he just started recording this week." There was a long moment—during which Ana could do little more than frown and rock. And then Gillian asked, "You didn't know?"

The hint of pity—or maybe blatant curiosity in Gillian's voice snapped Ana out of it.

"I knew he was in the studio." That was strictly true. Throughout his time in Vista Del Mar, Ward had spent significant time at a recording studio in L.A. "He produces albums. He's working on an album for some kid he heard in a club a few months ago."

"Yeah," Gillian said. "Dave Summers. He *was* working on his album. But they finished in the studio two weeks ago. Ward still had studio time and he's been using it himself."

Still not quite believing what she was hearing, she said, "You just called the studio and asked? And they told you?"

"I can be very persuasive." Gillian's voice was smugly pleased.

"Apparently," Ana grumbled.

"Look," Gillian began. "I'm sorry if I put my foot in it. If he's planning some big romantic gesture…" She let her voice trail off.

Yeah. Right. If Ward was planning some big romantic gesture, Ana would be arriving at the street festival in a chariot pulled by exotic long-haired llamas.

Still, Ana found herself offering up reassurances. "If he is planning something, I'll act surprised."

Which would not be hard to fake.

Whatever Ward was planning, it wasn't a gesture. Romantic, big or otherwise. They hadn't spoken since the fight at her uncle's house. All her life, she'd told herself she was putting off romance because the time wasn't right or because she hadn't yet met the right man. But maybe it was none of those things. Maybe she just sucked at love.

By the time Saturday rolled around, she no longer knew what to expect from the festival. Lena had showed up for work, on time, appropriately dressed and brimming with energy every day. She seemed not just determined to succeed, but to trample into the dust any doubts Ana might have had about her capabilities. She was even respectful. Mostly. She refrained from making snide comments about Ana unless they were alone. Christi and Omar were happy for the extra help in preparing for the street fair and agreed hiring Lena was a stroke of brilliance. Plus, the extra help had freed up Ana's time and allowed her to make progress on all the paperwork that had been bearing down on her.

There were even several minutes of each day leading up to the festival during which Ana didn't feel overwhelmed by the task ahead of her. Then she would remember the possibility that Ward would show up, and the panic would return.

But the night before she'd walked away from her job in L.A., her mother had reminded her that the things in life that most scared you were the only things worth doing. The street fair definitely felt like that. Terrifying, but worth the risk.

Midway through the schedule of events, Rafe was supposed to put in a brief appearance. Ana was glad of that. Before he left for Charleston, apparently Ward had done his best to convince Rafe to show up. Though Rafe's secretary had confirmed he'd be there and even though Emma spoke to him the previous day, Ana knew she'd relax considerably once his appearance was done with.

Just knowing he'd be there ratcheted up her own tension. Which was already high enough that she could barely sit still and hadn't eaten all day, despite the array of tempting treats the Bistro had provided.

Several local restaurants had set up booths on either side of the street where they were selling food. Naturally, all the proceeds would go to Hannah's Hope. In addition to the food, there were half a dozen performers scattered up and down the street, all people Ana had known during her stint in Hollywood. A couple of jugglers and a clown. In front of the police station, a couple of stunt men were giving demonstrations on how to fake a barroom brawl.

Ana had also talked some of her friends who were makeup artists into doing face painting for the kids. Even Emma's cousin, Becca Worth, had come down from Napa to offer up wine tastings. And all up and down the street, Christi, Omar and Lena were mingling, clipboards in hand, to recruit future volunteers and hand out pamphlets about the many resources Hannah's Hope could provide.

Watching it all, Ana felt a deep sense of satisfaction that almost—*almost*—replaced her sorrow. She relaxed only marginally when she saw Emma making her way through the crowd to her side. Chase was with her, a protective hand at her waist.

"This turnout is amazing!" Emma said loudly to be heard over the carnival atmosphere of the crowd. She leaned in to give Ana a hug of encouragement.

Ana returned it briefly and tried not to cling too long. "I know," she agreed, pressing a hand to her belly to calm her nerves. "I don't think I even knew there were this many people in town."

Emma gave a little frown. "Well, I'm guessing not. Don't you think a lot of people came in from San Diego? Even from L.A."

Something about Emma's tone sent Ana's anxiety soaring. "Why would they?"

Emma blanched. "I thought you knew. Didn't you see the paper today?"

"Which paper?" she asked, her dread tightening.

"All of them, I think." Emma gave Chase a nudge in the belly. "Can you pull it up on your phone?"

A few seconds later, Chase handed over his cell phone. Ana turned the phone and the headline from the *Gazette* popped into view. Ward Miller's Big Comeback, the headline read. She quickly scanned the article, which contained details about the new album he was recording. And about his appearance at the Hannah's Hope street festival.

"It ran in the San Diego paper and the *Los Angeles Times*."

After scanning the article, Ana carefully handed the phone

back to Chase. She resisted the urge to hurl it across the street. She thought that was quite mature of her.

"He shouldn't have misled that reporter." She pressed her lips together, trying not to say nasty things about Ward in front of Chase, who was, after all, his friend. And then she considered how this would make Hannah's Hope look and she cursed him out loud, despite her good intentions.

Emma frowned in concern and Chase raised his eyebrows.

"He didn't even consider how bad this is going to make the rest of us look when he doesn't show up."

"What makes you think he isn't going to show?" Chase asked.

Ana rolled her eyes. "He left town on Monday. I haven't heard a word from him since. If he was going to show, he would have said something."

"Are you sure he didn't?" Chase prodded.

"Yes! I'm—" Then she broke off, suddenly unsure. Because the last they had talked about the street fair had been before their big blow up. She had asked him to leave, but had never said anything about not coming here. "I don't know."

Suddenly all her nerves about the street fair crystallized into a big knot of anxiety. She wasn't entirely sure if she could face him again so soon.

But before she could rally her defenses…or even better, leave… she noticed a hush falling over the crowd. Heads started turning and a murmur of excitement flowed up the street toward a spot across from the makeshift stage at the edge of the park. A few feet away from her, she heard a man mention Ward's name and point toward the stage. She strained onto her toes, but couldn't see anything over the crowd. If Ward was out there somewhere, she wouldn't know it until he was right on top of her.

Omar had worked all morning setting up the PA system for the remarks both she and Rafe would make just after noon. Since that was his milieu, she'd left it in his capable hands and hadn't given it a second thought. Studying it now, she had no way of judging if it was just a normal PA system or something more devious. Like a sound system with which a famous musician might stage his comeback.

She had to stifle a growl of annoyance. How dare he show up here? After almost an entire week of silence? After breaking her heart?

But before the thought could even form in her mind, the frenzy of excitement in the crowd peaked. The masses parted and there he was walking toward her.

Not really walking toward her, of course, but rather toward the stage. Dressed casually in jeans and an untucked white linen shirt, he looked much the same as he had the first day they'd met. His sunglasses were up on his head. His sleeves were rolled up to reveal the tanned strength of his arms.

His progress through the crowd was slow because he stopped to talk to nearly everyone who greeted him. His smile was broad, his eyes crinkling with friendly laughter. There was an air of glamour and mystery about him, despite how casually he was dressed. Maybe it was the sheer magnetism of his personality. Maybe it was simply the way everyone he walked past responded to his presence. Whatever it was, she felt the tug of it herself, deep inside. Buried safe in her heart where no else would ever know it.

And she pushed that feeling even deeper, drawing on the nervous energy that had fueled her for the past week to muster up all the indignation she could.

She quickly excused herself from Emma and Chase and made her way through the crowd toward him. She was still too far away to overhear his words to the people who were stopping him—but she could all too easily imagine the fawning—when Jess stepped up beside him and spoke briefly into his ear. He nodded, then excused himself and made a beeline for the stage. She intercepted him at the steps.

When he spotted her, his expression shifted from the friendly, aren't-I-a-nice-guy-even-though-I'm-a-star smile to something more reserved. More carefully contained.

She doubted anyone would even notice the subtle change, but it pierced her heart.

Well, two could play that game. She propped her hands on her hips and looked at him with a cocked eyebrow. She blocked his path and stood close enough to keep their conversation from interested ears. "What are you doing here?"

"I would have thought that was obvious. The article in the *Gazette* said I'd take the stage at eleven to say a few words and maybe play a song or two."

She scowled. "I thought you weren't going to come."

His lips curved in a smile that was gently chiding. "Apparently, you don't read the papers."

Fourteen

His smile turned dangerously cocky. Like he knew a secret that she didn't. Like he still had some trick up his sleeve. It was an expression that made her very, very nervous. "If you don't want to hear me sing, I suggest you go inside. There are a lot of other people who would be disappointed if I don't. Besides, it's great publicity for Hannah's Hope."

She scanned the crowd, assessing the mood of all the people around her. He was right. Of course he was. Besides, every dollar people spent here today was going straight into Hannah's Hope's coffers. And whatever problems she may have with him personally, she knew he'd do a fine job of getting out the right message about the charity.

Still it was with grim resignation that she stepped aside and let him take the stage.

He trotted up the steps and raised a hand to wave at the people on the street. The crowd went wild, energized with sudden excitement. His stride was long and confident as he walked across the stage to the microphone. The very air around him seemed to vibrate with excitement.

She felt the pull of his allure deep in her gut. Was she crazy? There was something so…magnetic about him. For a second, watching him on stage, she honestly couldn't remember any of the reasons why they'd fought.

So what if he'd never really let her into his heart? So what if the lion's share of his affection was permanently locked away in his grief? What did any of that matter if she got to be with him?

And then she felt a curious little tug in her heart and she knew that it did matter. She was already in love with him. Time would only make it worse. Her decision may have been cowardly, but it was the only one she could make.

She forced her attention back to the stage, forced herself to listen to what he was saying. He'd already welcomed the crowd and made a laughing promise that he would play a new song—after he said a few words about Hannah's Hope.

"By now you all know that Hannah's Hope is about providing basic adult education for the people who need it most." His voice resonated through the crowd. He was a powerful speaker, giving the impression that his attention was focused on each and every member of the audience. "While Cameron Enterprises is fully committed to funding Hannah's Hope financially, this is not a problem money alone can solve. Funding can only do so much. We've got the money and the resources. Now we need your help."

He went on for several more minutes, delivering a rousing speech about the need for volunteers to mentor people and, more important, the need for clients to step forward and use the resources that Hannah's Hope could provide.

Despite that concern still nipping at the back of her mind, it was hard not to catch the excitement coursing through the crowd. She could tell from the expressions on the faces around her. Ward wasn't just drumming up interest in Hannah's Hope, he was inspiring commitment. He was convincing people of what she'd known all along. For Hannah's Hope to work, the entire community had to step up, together, to invest in their own future.

Today was the start of that. And together they would all make a difference.

"Hannah's Hope," he was saying, "is really about hope." His gaze seemed to search her out, meeting hers despite the distance and the hundreds of people around. "The hope that we can have a future together. If only we're willing to work for it."

Her heart tightened in her chest and she found herself blinking against the sting of tears.

"There's one person I met here in Vista del Mar that helped me learn that lesson in a very personal way. I'd like that person to join me up on stage for a minute."

Her breath caught in her throat while she waited for him to say her name. But it wasn't her name he called out.

"Ricky Cruz. Ricky, can you come on up?"

In a flash, Ricky dashed up the steps. He was dressed more nicely that she'd ever seen him, having abandoned his baggy faux gangster clothes for chinos and a dress shirt.

Ana cocked an eyebrow. Obviously, this had been staged.

"I've been mentoring Ricky here for the past couple of weeks. Not only has he made a commitment to me to stay in school, but he's personally taught me a lot. He even helped me work out a few kinks in this song I'm about to play." The crowd gave a laugh, clearly charmed by the way Ward was humoring Ricky. "So I can personally attest to the benefits of being a mentor."

Ward continued talking, explaining that the song he was going to play could be downloaded from iTunes and that all the proceeds from the sale of the song would go to Hannah's Hope. As Ward talked, Ricky pulled a stool forward from the corner of the stage. And then, seemingly out of nowhere, he pulled out a guitar and handed it to Ward.

Ward settled onto the stool, his left foot still on the ground, his right foot on the lowest rung of the stool. He slung the guitar strap over his shoulder, resting the guitar on his right knee.

She felt as though her heart had stopped beating.

It was the Alvarez.

She would have recognized its worn golden cedar anywhere.

She squeezed her eyes closed, emotion suddenly choking her.

A hush fell over the crowd. She wasn't the only one who recognized the famous Alvarez, but she may have been the only one to fully understand how difficult this was for him. Then she noticed Chase giving Emma's shoulder a squeeze, so maybe she wasn't the only one.

He reached up and adjusted the microphone so it was right next to his mouth. He barely had to look up to speak into it. "How's that sound?"

The crowd roared its approval.

He played a couple of notes, then twisted the tuner. Repeated the procedure. A few notes, an adjustment. Another few notes. Just a guy sitting on a stage with a guitar. Then he slipped seamlessly into the melody of the song.

He played for a few minutes without singing. His fingers moved easily over the strings of the guitar, coaxing out the song. The tune was complex and layered, full of yearning and emotion. If you weren't watching him play, you'd never guess it was just one guy, with one guitar. Somehow he made that Alvarez sound like an entire band.

Ana watched his intensity and concentration. Her heart was in her throat. This was what he was meant to do. What he was created for. Everything else in his life was just biding his time until he could get back to the guitar.

The song he played was a new one. Completely unfamiliar to her, and she'd heard every one of his songs at some point or another. A preternatural hush had fallen over the audience as they listened to the haunting and lovely melody.

Then his finger slipped and he played a wrong note.

He tilted his head just lightly so the audience could see his grin. "Sorry. Bit out of practice."

Everyone chuckled.

He slipped so easily back into the song, she wondered if he'd done it on purpose. Still playing, he starting speaking into the microphone. Just chatting as his fingers continued their complex fret work the way another man might drum his fingers on the table.

"When I was writing this song," he said, matching the rhythm of his words to the natural rhythm of the song. "I got some advice from my friend, Ricky. You remember Ricky, right?"

Ricky had moved to sit on the edge of the stage, his legs dangling off.

"Ricky asked, 'It isn't gonna be cheesy like your other songs, is it?'" The crowd groaned in response. Ricky gave a little wave to go with his sheepish smile. Ward mocked an expression of shock. "'What?' I said. And then he said, 'Dude, you sound like a—'" Ward broke off, gave the crowd a scan and then added, "Well, I'm not going to repeat the word he used. But then he told me, "You're a guy. No wonder she didn't believe you loved her if you talked like that.'"

Another laugh went through the crowd and Ward gave a little self-effacing shrug. "So here it is. A love song. Written by a guy. Just trying to convince a girl he really loves her. Here it is. 'Not Enough Words.'"

The haunting and lovely melody was in such sharp contrast to its simple words. There was a playfulness to the song, a humor his earlier songs had lacked. And still, there on his expression was the pure joy at playing.

The song was about how difficult it was to describe love. The lyrics were remarkably unfussy, a little self-deprecating. As if he couldn't really believe himself worthy of his shot at love. They lacked the poetic grace of some of his earlier songs, but she got the feeling that was intentional. Over and over again he repeated the refrain: *If I could tell you how much I loved you, you wouldn't believe me anyway.*

The song trailed off. For a moment, every person within earshot seemed to be holding their breath. And then the crowd went wild with approval.

Despite her own stunned and battered emotions, Ana found herself clapping along with everyone else. How could she not? The song was brilliant. It would be a hit. It would make so much money for Hannah's Hope, they may never need Rafe's support again. They may not even need the fundraiser, even though the planning for it was well underway. Besides, when it came to charitable foundations, there was no such thing as too much money.

On the other hand, the money from this song would trickle in for the rest of the time she worked at Hannah's Hope. It would always be there. A constant reminder of the love she'd turned away. Not that she needed reminding.

It took Ward thirty minutes to even get off the stage. Another twenty to make it out onto the street. Reporters were snapping pictures. People wanted autographs or just to shake his hand. He felt like he heard five hundred people say, "Great song, man," while he shook their hand. He didn't begrudge them—how could he?—and he appreciated the positive feedback. But in truth, there was only person he wanted to talk to. Only one opinion that mattered.

He knew she'd heard the song. After he'd taken the stage, she'd moved to a spot maybe thirty feet into the crowd. He met her gaze over the sea of people and it had been all he could do not to leap down off the stage and go to her. Screw the public performance. Forget the big gesture. But he needed her to hear the song. Needed her to know how he felt about her. Moreover, he needed her to have this experience. If he could win her back—and he hoped to God that he could—if they were going to be together, he needed her to know what it was like to have their relationship paraded about on the stage.

So despite how desperate he was to know how she felt, he didn't rush to her side, but slowly made his way through the crowd. He kept an eye on her though as she muttered a few words to Emma and Chase and then excused herself. She wended her way through the throng of people, and then disappeared through the front door of Bistro by the Sea, which was where Omar had told him they'd set up command central for the fair.

When he saw her slip through the door, he picked up the pace. He didn't want her getting out the back unnoticed.

He was relieved to find the restaurant largely empty. Faint sounds of cooking and cleanup drifted into the front room from the kitchen, but Ana was the only one in the dining room. She sat at a table, stacks of flyers spread out in front of her.

He waited until she looked up and then asked, "So what'd you think?"

Ana's gaze darted away from his and she tucked her hair behind her ears. "I think you—" Then she broke off and gave a little laugh. "I think you can write a good song. But you already knew that."

"Ana—" he took a step toward her, but she kept talking, warding off his approach.

"Donating the proceeds is incredibly generous. I'm sure we'll do so much good with the money. I'll make sure we do." Finally, she looked up at him. "But this changes nothing. You have to know that."

He bit back a curse.

"But I am glad—" her voice broke and she swallowed before continuing "—that you're playing the Alvarez again. It was time."

A sudden rush of anger hit him. "You know, Ana, all your theories about the Alvarez and the house…you know that's all crap, right?"

She blinked. He barely registered her surprise before charging on.

"And to be honest, I'm a little tired of you making unilateral assessments about my life, about my emotional state and about our relationship without even discussing them with me." He softened his harsh words with a smile, making sure she heard the gentle teasing behind them.

"What are you saying?" she arched a brow.

"I'm saying maybe you're not always right. Maybe the fact that I didn't play the Alvarez or sell the house had nothing to do with how I felt about Cara. Or whether or not I was over her death."

Her chin came up defensively, but she replicated his chiding tone. "Okay then, here's a shocking suggestion. Why don't you talk about your emotions for a change? 'Cause unless you tell me how you're feeling, it's kind of hard for me to know."

He flashed her a smile. "Didn't you hear the song? I'm a guy. We don't talk about our emotions."

She propped her hands on her hips. "So that's your excuse?"

Okay, apparently the charm wasn't going to work here. "No," he admitted, suddenly serious. "It's just always been easier with music."

She rolled her eyes. "Well, there are millions of men all around the world who manage to communicate their feelings just fine and they don't have the benefit of being world-renowned songwriters. So, dig a little deeper, okay?"

Damn it. He shoved a hand through his hair. He knew he needed to say this, but that didn't make it any easier. "No one has once bothered to ask me why I haven't sold the house."

She straightened, surprise flickering over her expression. "Why haven't you sold the house?"

"Honestly? I don't know what to do with it."

"I...what?"

"You want the truth? That's it. I have no idea how to get rid of it. You're so convinced I'm not over her death. Maybe you're right. I don't know how to get over anyone's death. I don't know how people just pick up and move on." He tipped up her chin, making her look him in the eye.

Because if he was going to do this, he was only going to do it once.

"You want the God's honest truth about my relationship with Cara? I loved her. I really did, but she didn't love me. Sure, at first, she did. She fell in love with the rock star. Ended up married to a mere man. An imperfect, completely human guy. At first, she didn't mind so much. We made it work. But once she was diagnosed, the illusion crumbled. She pulled back from the relationship. We never recovered. Why do you think she devoted so much of the last years of her life to charity work? Being married to me just wasn't enough for her."

Ana stood up. They were standing mere inches apart.

"Ward, I—"

"I just don't want to make the same mistake twice. I don't

want yet another woman stuck with me and unsure how to get out of the relationship."

"That wouldn't—"

"I'm not an easy man to love, Ana. I'm not about to ask you to make a commitment until you know for sure what you're getting into. You fell in love with the rock star and—"

She pressed her fingers to his lips to cut off his words. "You keep saying that, but it's just not true. I can't speak for Cara, maybe it was true for her, but it certainly isn't for me. I didn't even meet Ward Miller the musician until today. He's not the guy I fell in love with. I fell in love with Ward Miller the humanitarian. I fell in love with the guy who's devoted the past three years of his life to making a difference in the world. The guy who works so hard so that other people can follow their dreams. The guy who does all that and still finds time to mentor a needy kid. Maybe Ward Miller the rock star is buried somewhere in all of that. I don't know. I guess I'll just have to find out. Now that I've encouraged you to start playing again, I'm kind of stuck with him, aren't I?"

He smiled, slowly, letting the full implication of her words sink in before asking, "Are you? Stuck with Ward Miller, the musician?"

She searched his face. "I want to be. Of course I want to be. But I don't want half measures. I don't want only part of you. And I don't want to share you with her."

"You won't be," he assured her. And for the first time, he realized how true that was. Whatever love he'd had for Cara, it would always be a part of him, but it was a part of his past.

He cradled Ana's face in his hands and leaned down, gently pressing his lips to hers. He wanted to show her his love in that moment, but she would have none of his tenderness. She pulled him to her, opening her mouth beneath his. There was no playfulness in her kiss, no gentle exploration. There was only passion and urgency and longing.

When he finally pulled back, he knew he needed to offer her one more chance to walk away, or at the very least to negotiate terms. "If I'm going to do this—stage a comeback, I mean—it's not going to be easy. There will be long hours in the studio. Probably a tour. And I'd need you to come with me."

Her brow furrowed as she considered, but she nodded. "Okay."

"And some of the songs are going to be about you. About us. Having your life up there on stage, for everyone to see, it's not easy. I need to know you're okay with that."

She pulled his head down for another kiss. "I'll make it work. Besides, I have it on good authority that it's easier for men to express their emotions through music. Besides, I'm pretty fond of your guitar playing." She swallowed back the tears that threatened to choke her, then added, "That new song isn't half-bad, either."

He bumped her forehead with his own. "I may not say this enough. But I love you. Love you like crazy. And the thought of losing you scares me more than the thought of never recording another album. More than the thought of giving up the Alvarez forever. If being with you meant choosing to give up music forever, I'd pick you."

"I'm not going to ask you to do that."

"Thank God. 'Cause I really liked being back up on the stage." He leaned down and bumped his forehead against hers. "Thank you for pushing me. I needed that. I needed you."

Which she figured was just about perfect. Because she needed him, too.

* * * * *

Can Rafe Cameron's desire for revenge against the Worths be traced back to a fateful Valentine's Day fourteen years ago? Turn the page for an exclusive short story by USA TODAY bestselling author Catherine Mann. And look for the next installment in THE TAKEOVER *miniseries,* REVEALED: HIS SECRET CHILD *by Sandra Hyatt, wherever Silhouette books are sold.*

Vista del Mar, California—14 years ago:

Whoever decided flowers made the perfect Valentine's Day gift never spent backbreaking hours at a greenhouse shoveling manure.

Muscles shouting, Rafe Cameron scraped the remaining muck from the truck bed and walked to the pile five feet away behind the Worth family's glassed nursery. Sweat soaked his back and beaded his brow even in the fifty-five degree February weather. He'd ditched his pullover straight away, good thing since now his T-shirt and jeans were caked in filth.

But he was lucky to find a job to make extra money before school since afternoons were already filled with work at the construction company. Money was tight and he needed the additional cash to treat Sarah to a real Valentine's Day, a dinner out at that new fancy place in town, Jacques'. Not some cheapskate date like the ones they'd gone on over the past month.

Ice cream at the beach—then making out.

Sodas while driving around—followed by making out.

Free concert at the park—and more making out.

Rafe speared the shovel into the pile and leaned on the wooden handle to catch his breath. Hell, it was a wonder he had time for a girlfriend to give flowers to, anyway. He hadn't meant to start dating Sarah Richards, but then he'd kissed her that night a month ago when he'd picked her up from her job waitressing at the snobby Beach and Tennis Club.

Now here he was, working for that scumbag Ronald Worth, the richest dude in Vista del Mar. At least he didn't have to see Worth. Technically, he'd gotten the job from Worth's gardener, Juan Rodriguez.

Still, his senior English teacher would call this short-term job the ultimate in "irony" since he'd always sworn nothing would make him kowtow to Worth's millions. Except he'd started dating Sarah, which changed a lot of things fast.

Funny what a guy would do for a girl, but then it must run in his genes. His dad had sure worked his tail off to pay medical bills piled higher than the fertilizer reeking up the morning air… not that it had mattered in the end since she'd died anyway. Hannah. His mother. And now his dad had started up a *friendship* with Penny.

Rafe threw back his head and stared at the cobalt-blue morning sky until the sun burned away the lame moisture in his eyes.

Focus on the right now. Besides money for a date, he needed a proper Valentine's bouquet to give Sarah when she got off work tonight. The job was doubly perfect in that Mr. Rodriguez had offered to wrap up some flowers as part of the pay.

The gardener—a middle-aged, Zen kinda dude—clapped him on the back. "*Niño,* you have worked enough this week. Go shower up before you are late for school. As I tell my little Ana, education is important."

"I agree, sir." His dad hammered the same thing into his head often enough.

"The flowers of your choice will be wrapped and waiting with floral tubes of water on their stems. But make sure you keep them cool, in your refrigerator when you go home to shower."

"Thank you for helping me out with this job and letting me

come in so early." He peeled off the disgusting glove and shook the older man's hand. "I won't forget it."

"No thanks are necessary. You are a hard worker. Do the same favor for someone else someday. That is how the world should move, people helping each other out, helping each other find fulfillment and happiness in the moment." Rodriguez reached into his pocket and pulled out a check.

Rafe stared at the Worth Industries label scrolling across the top, a company that had once carried his parents on their payroll, a company that fired his parents unfairly, taking away their income, their health insurance, their future.

He fought hard against the urge to crumple the slip of paper. "I won't forget."

Damn straight, he had a long memory, as Ronald Worth would one day find out.

Rafe's hair was wet and she wanted to touch it.

In the high school parking lot, Sarah sat in the front seat of Rafe's El Camino, making the most of the final five minutes before the bell rang. Her fingers itched to stroke over his damp, swept-back hair, a darker shade, almost brown when saturated with water. Threading her fingers through his thick hair was such a turn-on.

Okay, everything about Rafe was a total turn-on.

Happiness sang through her veins. It was the best Valentine's Day ever and she wanted to soak in every second. Even though it was basically a day like any other at Vista del Mar High, everything seemed crisper, brighter. Details, she wanted to remember each and every one.

A sophomore couple wove through cars, arms around each other in spite of the ban on PDAs on school property. A trio of basketball cheerleaders raced past, carrying boxes of heart-shaped lollipops for a Valentine's Day fundraiser.

Officer G drove his cruiser slowly in front of the brick school, always on the lookout for drugs. And if he couldn't find those, he seemed just as content to nab anybody going two miles per hour over the speed limit. Yep, it was a school day like any other—except school wasn't half as boring these days. Since Rafe. She snuggled deeper into the seat that smelled like Rafe... and something else.

Frowning, she sniffed again, confused by what teased her nose. "Your car smells like perfume."

He raised an eyebrow, lazy, slowlike. "Are you accusing me of cheating on you? Because honest to God, Sarah, I don't know when I would find the time."

"Are you accusing me of being jealous?" And maybe she was a little. The thought of him being with anyone else made her chest hurt.

"I don't have time for games either, Sarah." His blue eyes went sort of cold.

Rafe sure didn't have much of a sense of humor, but he'd said one time that it worked out okay since a smile from her chased away his bad mood.

So she smiled now, enjoying the way she could make him happy. "And yes, I also know you don't have time for another girl."

"Good." He smiled back.

She gave into temptation and skimmed her fingers over his damp hair. She still couldn't believe she had the right to do this anytime she wanted. A shiver of excitement skipped down her spine. His blue eyes lit with a look she recognized well from make-out sessions on Busted Bluff.

Swallowing hard, she pulled her hand away before they started necking in the high school parking lot and got busted for real— and not on the bluff. "I was just curious if maybe your dad used your El Camino for a date."

His grin faded along with the light in his eyes. "He didn't use my truck and he doesn't date."

"Not even Penny?"

"They're friends and they spend time together, but it's not really dating," he insisted with too much force.

Abruptly, he opened his door and stepped out into the parking lot packed with teenage-style wheels and students rushing toward the concrete steps.

Rather than wait for him to open her door the way he always insisted on doing, she leapt out after him, hauling her backpack hooked on her elbow by one strap. Guilt stung and blood rushed to her face. She shouldn't have been so pushy. But he didn't talk about himself much and she wanted to get closer, to understand him better.

Sarah met him in front of the hood, dropping her backpack to the ground so she could hold his face in her hands. "I'm sorry."

"Don't apologize," he said brusquely.

Her fingers slid away from his cheeks. She leaned back against the car watching him go all moody on her, and she sensed a smile alone wasn't going to chase away his frown.

She wanted to tell him to lighten up and enjoy Valentine's Day. But right now wasn't about her. It was about him. "It must be tough seeing your dad with somebody else."

He stayed quiet, his shoulders tensed and braced under his denim jacket.

"I can't imagine how I would be if something happened to my mom or my grandmother." Even thinking about it made her throat close up for a second. Sure his mom had died three years ago, but she wasn't sure a person could ever totally get over losing a family member. At least she would have people to turn to for comfort and sharing memories if someone she loved died. "You don't have a lot of people to depend on since your mom passed."

His stony jaw flexed as if he was chewing over her words. "Sorry doesn't mean much when you turn right around and do the same thing all over again."

Anger edged aside her sympathy. She came by her red hair honestly, with a temper to match. Sometimes she could control it, sometimes not. She clenched her teeth together for a second, holding back the urge to snap at him.

Three heartbeats later, she took a deep breath. "You're being grouchy because I upset you. I really am sorry, and if you knew me at all you would realize that I didn't mean any harm. I was just trying to help."

He hooked a finger in the loose silky scarf looped around her neck and tugged her closer. "Is that an offer to soothe my hurting heart?"

"Argh!" She punched his shoulder, temper winning out. "God, Rafe. Don't be a jerk. It's Valentine's Day. And I'm trying to be understanding here, but Valentine's Day is supposed to be all about the girlfriend."

"You're really pretty when you get fired up like that."

His words stopped her tirade dead in its tracks.

"Oh," she said. *Brilliant.*

He eyed her with that steamy look that sent shivers up and down her spine until she ached to climb in the back of his El Camino and make out on a blanket under the stars. And just that fast, he clamped his hands around her waist and plopped her down to sit on the hood of his car. *Yum!*

The chatter and revving engines in the parking lot faded as her world zeroed in on Rafe. What would his hands feel like against the bare flesh under her sweater? Under her bra. They'd had some heavy-duty make-out sessions and he'd touched her—there—with her clothes between them, not that he would have been able to miss just how crazy he made her as she went all tight from his touch. Her breasts tingled even now just thinking about all the time they'd spent at Busted Bluff.

Her skin went hotter than from any embarrassed flush. He stepped closer until his legs pressed against hers, denim to denim. He could be a model in one of those bad-boy faded jeans commercials and she would buy out the store. Her emotions were all roller coaster careening inside her, but then that seemed pretty much the norm around Rafe.

She leaned forward, nibbling her bottom lip in anticipation.

Thump. The sound echoed, jolting her upright. She looked left fast—at Quentin Dobbs from English class and work.

Quentin's backpack dragged along the side of Rafe's El Camino. "Sorry. Didn't mean to scratch your paint."

Rafe angled away, placing his body between her and Quentin. "Really, Dobbs, do you think I would even notice?"

"Yeah, right, I guess so." He glanced from Sarah to Rafe,

then back again. "Bell's gonna ring in a second. You don't want to get a detention and be late for work at the restaurant. See you inside."

She watched him walk away, feeling bad about things she couldn't change.

Rafe draped his arm over her shoulder. "He has a crush on you."

"I know." She pulled her eyes off her classmate and back to Rafe. "But it's harmless. He's a nice, good-looking guy. He'll find somebody else."

"Nice, good-looking guy?" He stared down at her intently. "Maybe I'm the one who should be jealous."

As if. "Do you see me wearing his school ring?"

"You're not wearing mine, either." His jaw flexed again so hard she worried he would crack a tooth over the fact that he didn't have a high school ring to give her.

"Stop with the money thing, okay? I'm with *you*. The day you see me wearing his ring—" she rolled her eyes, certain that would never happen "—then you can worry."

That night, Rafe stood on the front doorstep of Sarah's mustard-yellow stucco house, flowers behind his back, his jaw just about on the ground. "You look amazing."

And she did. Her red hair was loose, how he liked it most. She'd curled it, though, until it danced all around her face, on her shoulders and down her back the way he wanted to touch her. She wore a silky dress the same shade of green as her eyes, like the leaves on the exotic plants in the greenhouse. Over her shoulders, she had a black sweater with some kind of silver threads in it that winked like the stars.

She was all prettied up and as much as he enjoyed looking at her, he hated that his change in plans tonight might disappoint her. But he didn't have any choice. For a minute, though, he just wanted to memorize the smile on her face.

Her grandmother—the old battle-ax didn't like him, which chapped his hide since she seemed to like everyone else in town—stood behind her granddaughter with narrow eyes and a tight frown. "Have her home before midnight. Just because her parents work the late shift doesn't mean she can run around town doing whatever she wants."

"Yes, ma'am." He put on his best manners, for Sarah's sake.

Grouchy granny Kathleen Richards hugged her granddaughter, whispering something in her ear. No doubt something bad about him. Kathleen worked as Ronald Worth's assistant, so she wasn't particularly high up on Rafe's list of favorite people, either. But he would do whatever it took to wrangle his way into her good graces since that was the key to Grandma Kat loosening the reins when Sarah wasn't at work.

The two Richards women kept their heads close together. Kathleen's was the same color of red but cut short and with some silver in it, kinda like the threads in Sarah's sweater. Finally, Grandma Kat finished whatever it was she had to say and stepped back.

He pulled his left hand out from behind his back, with a pink tulip in his fist. "For you, ma'am. Happy Valentine's Day."

Kathleen's green eyes lit with surprise, then suspicion. Still, she smiled politely enough. "Thank you, young man. That's very thoughtful of you. But you still have to have her home by midnight."

Nodding, Rafe laughed lightly. "Of course."

Sarah stepped out on the front porch, closing the door behind her. "Sorry about that. Grandma Kat is just overprotective."

"I'm glad you have someone watching out for you when your parents are working late." True enough. Between him and Grandma Kat, they made sure Sarah didn't do something reckless like walk home by herself from work.

"Yeah, well, she's never been the kind of person to hide what she's feeling." Sarah tugged the sweater around her arms, the night breeze lifting her curls. "She may be feisty, but she's up front and honest."

"Like her granddaughter." Although thank God the granddaughter seemed to like him more than the grandmother.

"Thank you. I'll take that as a compliment."

She tugged the tie that he'd borrowed from his dad. His dad's only jacket hadn't fit though, so Rafe was stuck with just a shirt and work khakis to go with it.

"As long as you're smiling, Sarah, I'm good with however you want to take it." He watched the way her green eyes grinned right along with her mouth. He lost track of how long he stared while the porch swing creaked in the wind.

Then she tipped her head to the side, curls swaying to the side. "What else is behind your back?"

He pulled his fist around in front of him, clutching the bouquet full of flowers, most of which he didn't even know the names of, but it looked like a burst of color with pinks, yellows, purples and reds. It was freaking huge and he probably owed Mr. Rodriguez extra work for all of this. But he wasn't one bit sorry when he saw the way Sarah's eyes lit up.

"Oh, Rafe!" she squealed and her feet did a speedy, impromptu tap dance on the wooden porch. She gave him a quick kiss, then gathered up the flowers to her nose, inhaling deeply.

She moaned with a pleasure that made his groin pull tight as he imagined other ways to bring the kittenish sound from her throat. Or maybe it was the kiss that sent his pulse skyrocketing. Either way, he was one uncomfortable dude.

"Oh, Rafe!" she said again with an obvious excitement that couldn't be missed or faked. "These are amazing. I can't believe you did this, and ohmigosh, you are such a good secret keeper since you didn't even give me a hint all day."

"I'm glad you're happy."

"Very much so." She smiled at him over the flowers, the porch light playing with the hints of gold in her red hair. "Is this what I smelled in your car this morning?"

"You've got me there."

She scrunched her nose. "I can't believe I was such a jealous brat."

"I would feel the same if I thought you were seeing someone else." Rafe couldn't shake the image of how Quentin Dobbs had looked at her. He knew she wouldn't lie to him, but still. The guy liked her and didn't make any secret of it even though the whole world knew Sarah was dating Rafe.

Possessiveness pumped through his veins. Not smart. He prided himself on being calm, focused.

Sarah put her flowers on the porch swing as carefully as she placed an expensive dinner on the table at work. "I have something for you, too."

"You didn't have to do that. I seem to recall someone with the most amazing red hair and a smoking hot body telling me—just this morning—that Valentine's Day is for girls."

She flicked her hair over her shoulders with a sass that never failed to turn him inside out.

"And this girl wanted to get you something." She reached into her purse and withdrew a small gold gift bag. "Hope you like it."

He plucked through all the tissue paper, decorative white and clear, both flecked with gold to match the bag. He and his dad exchanged gifts on Christmas and birthdays, but they usually passed them over to each other in the plastic store bag. He hadn't had anything wrapped up like this since before his mom died.

Rafe pushed aside the last of the paper and found..."A money clip?"

Fat lot of use that was going to get. But he smiled anyway, fast, so as not to hurt her feelings.

"It's for all the millions you're going to make." She pulled the gold money clip from his hands and hooked it on his tie playfully. "And there's something else in there, too. Something little and maybe kinda silly, but I thought you would enjoy it."

He stuffed his hand inside, found something small and metallic. He pulled out...a Matchbox car, a black Porsche. Now that made him smile for real. She'd remembered how he talked about dreaming of owning one and driving it right down Main Street so fast that Officer G wouldn't even be able to catch him.

Rafe closed his fingers around the toy car and leaned forward to kiss her, lingering, knowing he should pull back for a bunch of reasons. Number one reason being that Battle-Ax Granny was on the other side of the door. But he'd been thinking about Sarah all day—and it had definitely been a long day that started way too early. So yeah, he wanted to take a few extra seconds to enjoy how soft her lips felt against his, the way she sighed as she kind of melted against his chest.

Her purse thudded to the porch and her sweater slid away. Her fingernails dug into his shoulders in a way he was starting to learn meant she was every bit as into this as he was. He cupped her neck to hold on to not just her, but the kiss a little longer. Fiery red curls brushed against the back of his wrist, softer than anything he could remember feeling. His hands itched to tangle up in her hair, have it all over him. Have her all over him. His blood pounded in his ears, demanding *more, more, more.*

His hands started shaking from restraint. He needed to cut this short before he lost control right here on her front porch, for crying out loud.

Pulling back, he sketched his fingers down Sarah's creamy smooth cheek. "Thank you. For both gifts. They're great. You're great."

And he really would have been wiser to leave her alone because he didn't have a clue where they could take this relationship once they graduated. But for tonight—for Valentine's Day, for Sarah—he would put the future aside and live in the moment. The way she did.

Sarah raked her fingernail along the toy Porsche's wheels, spinning the tiny tires. "Okay then, I guess we'd better get going or we'll be late for our reservation at Jacques'."

Damn it.

He'd forgotten the crummy news for a few minutes, distracted by her smile. By her mouth. By her.

When he'd come home to shower up after the greenhouse job, he'd found the power cut off in his house. He'd called his dad at work, and Bob had said he was late with the bill but would figure out a way to pay it on Monday. They would just have to take cold showers for the weekend. All would be fine.

But Rafe had known all wasn't *fine.* His dad was still trying to pay off the medical bills three years after Hannah died. From what Rafe could tell, his dad was barely paying the interest on the loans. Forget about making a dent in the principal.

Standing in the cold kitchen, Rafe had held the Worth Industries check in his hand, hating Ronald Worth all over again for the numerous ways he'd screwed up the Cameron family's lives. But at least today Worth's money could achieve something positive. Rafe had told his dad he had the extra cash and he would pay the power bill after school on his way to work at the construction company. A quick trip to the bank, and he'd had the money in hand to pay the electric company—Worth's checks were always honored on the spot at the bank, the teller had assured him.

At least he'd still had the flowers to give Sarah. Although it felt like poor consolation as he looked into her pretty glittering green eyes, realizing he couldn't even give her half of what she deserved…

Not tonight. And not even a few months from now when they both graduated.

But first he had to break the bad news to Sarah about their dinner plans.

* * * * *

COMING NEXT MONTH

Available March 8, 2011

#2071 HIS HEIR, HER HONOR
Catherine Mann
Rich, Rugged & Royal

#2072 REVEALED: HIS SECRET CHILD
Sandra Hyatt
The Takeover

#2073 BILLIONAIRE BABY DILEMMA
Barbara Dunlop
Billionaires and Babies

#2074 SEDUCING HIS OPPOSITION
Katherine Garbera
Miami Nights

#2075 ONE NIGHT WITH PRINCE CHARMING
Anna DePalo

#2076 PROMOTED TO WIFE?
Paula Roe

SDCNM0211

REQUEST YOUR FREE BOOKS!

2 FREE NOVELS
PLUS 2
FREE GIFTS!

Passionate, Powerful, Provocative!

YES! Please send me 2 FREE Silhouette Desire® novels and my 2 FREE gifts (gifts are worth about $10). After receiving them, if I don't wish to receive any more books, I can return the shipping statement marked "cancel." If I don't cancel, I will receive 6 brand-new novels every month and be billed just $4.05 per book in the U.S. or $4.74 per book in Canada. That's a saving of at least 15% off the cover price! It's quite a bargain! Shipping and handling is just 50¢ per book in the U.S. and 75¢ per book in Canada.* I understand that accepting the 2 free books and gifts places me under no obligation to buy anything. I can always return a shipment and cancel at any time. Even if I never buy another book, the two free books and gifts are mine to keep forever.

225/326 SDN FC65

Name	(PLEASE PRINT)	
Address		Apt. #
City	State/Prov.	Zip/Postal Code

Signature (if under 18, a parent or guardian must sign)

Mail to the **Reader Service:**
IN U.S.A.: P.O. Box 1867, Buffalo, NY 14240-1867
IN CANADA: P.O. Box 609, Fort Erie, Ontario L2A 5X3

Not valid for current subscribers to Silhouette Desire books.

Want to try two free books from another line?
Call 1-800-873-8635 or visit www.ReaderService.com.

* Terms and prices subject to change without notice. Prices do not include applicable taxes. Sales tax applicable in N.Y. Canadian residents will be charged applicable taxes. Offer not valid in Quebec. This offer is limited to one order per household. All orders subject to credit approval. Credit or debit balances in a customer's account(s) may be offset by any other outstanding balance owed by or to the customer. Please allow 4 to 6 weeks for delivery. Offer available while quantities last.

Your Privacy—The Reader Service is committed to protecting your privacy. Our Privacy Policy is available online at www.ReaderService.com or upon request from the Reader Service.

We make a portion of our mailing list available to reputable third parties that offer products we believe may interest you. If you prefer that we not exchange your name with third parties, or if you wish to clarify or modify your communication preferences, please visit us at www.ReaderService.com/consumerchoice or write to us at Reader Service Preference Service, P.O. Box 9062, Buffalo, NY 14269. Include your complete name and address.

SDES11

Start your Best Body today with these top 3 nutrition tips!

1. SHOP THE PERIMETER OF THE GROCERY STORE: The good stuff—fruits, veggies, lean proteins and dairy—always line the outer edges of the store. When you veer into the center aisles, you enter the temptation zone, where the unhealthy foods live.

2. WATCH PORTION SIZES: Most portion sizes in restaurants are nearly twice the size of a true serving and at home, it's easy to "clean your plate." Use these easy serving guidelines:
- Protein: the palm of your hand
- Grains or Fruit: a cup of your hand
- Veggies: the palm of two open hands

3. USE THE RAINBOW RULE FOR PRODUCE: Your produce drawers should be filled with every color of fruits and vegetables. The greater the variety, the more vitamins and other nutrients you add to your diet.

Find these and many more helpful tips in

YOUR BEST BODY NOW
by
TOSCA RENO
WITH STACY BAKER

Bestselling Author of
THE EAT-CLEAN DIET®